Fatal Puzzle

A THRILLER

CATHERINE SHEPHERD
Translated by Julia Knobloch

amazon crossing

Previously published by the author as *Der Puzzlemörder von Zons* in Germany in 2013. Translated from German by Julia Knobloch.

Published by AmazonCrossing, Seattle

www.apub.com

Amazon, the Amazon logo, and AmazonCrossing are trademarks of Amazon.com, Inc., or its affiliates.

ISBN-13: 9781477826508
ISBN-10: 1477826505

Cover design by Edward Bettison Ltd

Library of Congress Control Number: 2014910095

Printed in the United States of America

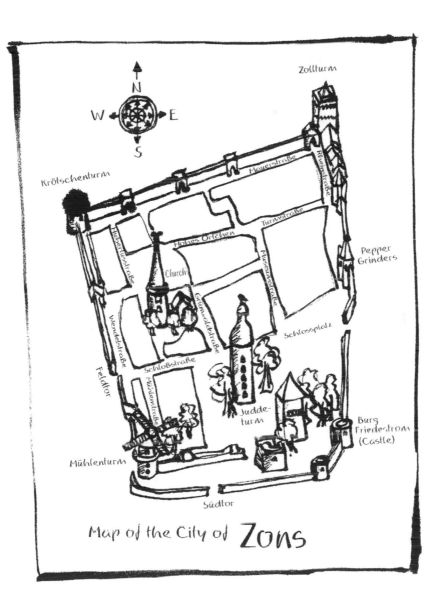

Map of the City of **Zons**

I.

Present

"When you're sad, look up at the stars, then close your eyes. The stars will tell you a story. Their soft gleam will embrace and comfort you and lead you confidently toward your goals."

Wandering through the streets of the small medieval town of Zons on a frigid winter's evening, Anna smiled as she remembered her grandfather's words. Although the icy air made her shiver, she sat down on one of the many benches along the bank of the Rhine. She thought about following her grandfather's advice, and tears filled her eyes.

No, she told herself sternly. She wouldn't let the pain overwhelm her for more than a brief moment. She didn't want to rehash the past any longer, didn't want to be reminded of the sorrows that had turned these last few months into a living hell—there was no other way of putting it. For weeks now she had tormented herself with a stream of self-pitying thoughts that she couldn't seem to banish. She was ready to look ahead and regain her equilibrium at last.

When would she be able to leave the past behind and move on with her usual poise and calm, easily mastering her life as she normally did? Granted, she'd never been one of those people who seemed to court good luck wherever they went—but she certainly couldn't complain of chronic misfortune, either. Well, except for the past few months, during which everything that had been dearly important to her had almost entirely vanished.

Taking her grandfather's advice, Anna turned her head toward the sky. Clouds were moving in quickly to cover the moon and stars, but for now the stars were so bright they almost blinded her. She stared up into the sky for several minutes and then closed her eyes. Gradually, her thoughts dissolved in the glistening bounty, and Anna felt herself lifted upward, her body nearly weightless. For a fleeting moment, the world around her fell away. As if drawn by a vision, Anna drifted deep into the night, engulfed in a bright gleam. She had no thoughts, no feelings. The tears in her eyes splintered the light into countless separate beams, leading Anna toward a glittering palace of shining rays. Perfect indifference flooded her body. If only this sensation would last forever!

·   ·   ·

Icy gusts of wind made Anna's body tremble and brought her back to earth. Snowflakes swirled in the air, draping her in a white veil. She must have fallen asleep. She wanted to rise quickly, but her stiff limbs ached with even the slightest movement. Her cozy apartment wasn't far; in less than ten minutes she could be comfortably back in her heated room, protected from this ghastly cold. She made herself stand and slowly trudged down the deserted street. The snow was falling so heavily now that she could barely see the tips of her shoes.

Suddenly she noticed a man's silhouette directly in front of her. She stopped abruptly and stared into the stranger's face; dark-brown eyes stared back at her. Blond strands of hair peeked from beneath his hood, and Anna could tell he was attractive.

"May I be of assistance? At this late hour it is rather dangerous for such a fair lady to be strolling about unaccompanied."

How old-fashioned his language is, Anna noted. "Oh, thank you," she said. "But I'm almost home. It won't take long."

He insisted nonetheless, and Anna, who usually made a point of not allowing a stranger to walk her home, accepted on a whim. They walked swiftly through the quiet cobblestone streets and soon reached Anna's building at Rheinstraße 4. He smiled when he said good-bye and disappeared into the darkness.

II.

Five Hundred Years Ago

The miller in Zons had six sons, the youngest and the smartest of whom was named Bastian. Tall and muscular, he would have made a great miller himself—but from an early age, Bastian was educated by the priest in reading and writing. The boy turned out to be a curious and intelligent student. Both Father Johannes and the commander of the City Guard were impressed by his talent for solving all kinds of mysteries and riddles. That was why Bastian was appointed to the City Guard's squadron at the beginning of the year 1495 and charged with dealing with murderers, con men, and other criminals.

Nestled between Cologne and Düsseldorf on the banks of the river Rhine, Zons had long been a small, peaceful village where not much of anything happened, let alone crime. But in 1372, almost a hundred years earlier, Archbishop Friedrich von Saarwerden of Cologne had authorized Zons to levy a toll on ships transporting cargo on the river—a privilege formerly held by the considerably larger neighboring town of Neuss. Only one year later, Saarwerden granted Zons its town charter. Things had never been the same since then. Criminals of all sorts invaded the city, suddenly bringing in dangers like muggings and robberies.

To better protect the city, the archbishop ordered a giant wall erected around the perimeter of Zons, complete with an impressive *Zollturm*—a toll tower transported from Neuss—and several other watchtowers. Viewed from above, the wall resembled a gigantic, right-angled trapezoid. Each corner featured at least one watchtower. Soon enough, the playful people of Zons took to calling them "pepper grinders." From the small windows in the upper stories of the towers, hot pitch and rocks could be scattered on the town's enemies like pepper.

The Zons mill was situated at the southwest corner of the city wall. From there, it was a short walk for Bastian to get to the small marketplace and the church, where he felt thoroughly at home. Over the years, the priest had become like a second father to him.

At only twenty-three, Bastian was already considered one of the most honorable citizens of Zons, and soon he would be a wedded man. Only a few weeks earlier he had finally dared to propose to his darling Marie, the baker's daughter who lived in the house right next to the huge Zollturm. Bastian and Marie had grown up together. Ever since he was a little boy, Bastian had known that one day Marie would be his wife.

. . .

Her head felt heavy, as if she had drunk a whole barrel of wine by herself, although she couldn't recall having drunk even a single goblet. A warm liquid ran over her face and mouth, and when she licked her dry, chapped lips she noticed a metallic taste. She tried to move her hands but couldn't. A wave of panic rushed through her body. She wanted to scream, but immediately a pair of stinking, coarse hands covered her mouth, muffling even the slightest sound. Where was she? Who was this reeking man? The last emotion Elisabeth would experience during her short life was astonishment.

. . .

Bastian was dreaming of his father's mill. The millstones were grinding loudly against each other. Then a roaring sound and a forceful throbbing reached the edge of his consciousness. Tons of pure, white flour thundered to the ground of the first floor, where workers poured it into huge linen sacks. Bastian lifted one of the bulging sacks on his strong shoulders and loaded it onto the horse-drawn cart waiting in front of the mill. The roaring of the grindstones grew louder and louder, and suddenly, the throbbing returned.

Something wasn't right. Hopefully the grinder hadn't broken. Abruptly, Bastian sat up and realized that he was not in the mill at all. It was dark, he was in bed, and he had been dreaming. Downstairs someone was hammering frantically against the door and calling his name. What was going on?

Suddenly Bastian was wide-awake. He hurried down the stairs to open the door and found Wernhart, his friend from the City Guard, panting and out of breath.

"We found Elisabeth. By God, hurry up, Bastian. She's dead—and mangled so badly I hardly recognized her."

With lightning speed, Bastian threw on his clothes and followed Wernhart. The two friends ran down Mühlenstraße and turned right into Schlossstraße, which led them to the segment of the city wall directly behind the *Schlossplatz*, the castle square.

Bastian saw what could easily be taken for a sagging flour sack dangling by a chain from the parapet of the watchtower. At second glance, though, he saw that it was a human body wrapped in a linen gown, hanging from one arm and idly swinging back and forth. A pair of tied-up feet peeped out from beneath the gown, and when a gust of wind blew off the hood that covered the body's head, Bastian recognized Elisabeth. All her hair had been shaved off. Her shoulder appeared to be dislocated, and her other arm wasn't visible.

Bastian's colleagues from the City Guard had already arranged for several torches. But even with their light and a bright, full moon, it was still too dark to examine the body.

"Take her off that chain at once!" Bastian called to the men from the City Guard. "Wernhart, go fetch the doctor. Tell him we'll be right here with Elisabeth. I want him to take a look at her and see if he can tell us what happened."

He thoroughly familiarized himself with the crime scene, and then he drew a little sketch of the victim and the chain in the first page of his new notebook. Why did such a catastrophe have to happen during his first three months on the job? Wasn't it up to him to make the city safer and to prevent such atrocities?

In the meantime, poor Elisabeth's body had been placed on the bed of a cart. Bastian approached her to take a better look. He knew he would have to wait until daylight to examine her more closely, but he held a torch above her body to assess what he could. Her hands and feet were dirty, and gruesome injuries covered her scalp, as if someone had carved a bloody pattern into it with a knife.

III.

Present

Emily could hardly believe her luck. She had gotten the job! She gazed at the gray envelope containing the contract. She was so happy she almost jumped up and down like a little girl. She was a pert and pretty young woman with deep brown eyes and curly, dark hair. Even on a normal day, Emily's smile and warmth could light up a small room; today she was positively radiant.

It might be only a small gig, but it was her first real one. She was in her last year of journalism school at Cologne University, and she had just been assigned to write an entire feature series for the daily newspaper the *Rheinische Post*. And what's more, the series would be about her favorite topic, the medieval Zons murder cases. While many journalists from the region would have preferred to write for the more prestigious *Handelsblatt* based in Düsseldorf, Emily had little interest in writing about finance; the quest for money and power was too dry for her taste. As an undergraduate she had majored in history, and when she decided to get a graduate degree in journalism, she knew that her interest in the past would somehow lead her to the most fascinating stories.

Emily had been riveted by her studies in medieval history and had even dedicated several years to studying old German handwriting and scriptures. Something about that dark and mystical era held a magical attraction for her. Even as a little girl she'd preferred playing with toy knights to Barbie and Ken. Every summer she used to spend a couple of weeks in Italy with her grandparents, who lived next to a Franciscan monastery in Assisi. Often she would visit the small medieval chapel on the monastery grounds to hear the monks praying.

She would have to tell her family the good news, but first she had to fill Anna in right away. Though her best friend wasn't in the best of spirits these days, Emily knew that Anna would certainly share her joy.

Poor Anna. A few months ago, she had finally mustered the courage to propose to her boyfriend, Martin, and that had triggered a huge catastrophe. First Martin asked Anna for three whole days to think it over. Then, at the end of those three days, he came out to Anna as gay, leaving her utterly devastated as well as perplexed. To make things almost tragically worse, Martin's lover turned out to be Christopher, Anna's and Emily's best friend.

The three had been close friends for years and spent a great deal of time together. In recent months, however, Christopher had gradually withdrawn from both Anna and Emily. The days of hours-long shopping trips and entire afternoons spent in coffeehouses, laughing about anything and everything, had dwindled to nothing. At first the two girls had thought Christopher must be lovesick, but he wasn't at all forthcoming whenever they tried to discuss his withdrawal from them. Eventually, they decided it was best to give him some space and leave him to his own devices. More and more often they went out without Christopher, but they never gave up hope that he would one day be a part of their lives again.

Now it turned out he was indeed a part of their lives, but in a way they could never have suspected and that injured one of their group to the core. Although Anna tried hard to pull herself together when Emily was around, her laughter seemed hollow and forced.

Emily had never particularly liked Martin and had always felt that Anna deserved someone better. But she hadn't seen this coming. At least the happy couple had moved to Berlin, where they hoped to indulge without restraint in their newfound bliss, so Anna and Emily didn't have to worry about running into them on a daily basis.

Emily fished around in her purse for her cell phone and called Anna. They decided to meet up later that afternoon at Anna's apartment in Zons, which worked out incredibly well for Emily. Anna's apartment was in a tiny house on the right side of the medieval Zollturm, which had been built in 1222 and later moved to Zons. Emily swiftly collected all her materials about the fifteenth-century murder cases. Betting she'd get the assignment, she had already begun her research and was now eager to examine the crime scenes more closely in light of what she'd learned.

She quickly skimmed her documents. The first victim had been one Elisabeth Kreuzer, age eighteen, who had lived in the house next door to the tower called the *Krötschenturm*, located in the northwest part of the small town. According to the records, her body had been found the night of December 15, 1495, by Wernhart Tillman, a local resident and member of the City Guard. Bastian Mühlenberg had been head of the investigation. The murder must have been extremely brutal; the young woman had been tortured, raped, and finally left dangling on an iron chain from the Krötschenturm. On her scalp, the investigators found a carving of symbols and letters that initially couldn't be deciphered. Emily knew that the county archive in Neuss still owned a copy of a sketch of that carving, together with other case-relevant documents. She simply had to get her hands on those papers. She would ask Anna to accompany her that afternoon to the Zons branch of the county archive, which was located at Schlossstraße 1.

IV.

Five Hundred Years Ago

His hands shook the way they always did when he thought of his father.

"Say the Lord's Prayer! Say it once more. Speak evenly and stop trembling, damn it!"

With every prayer, the whip in his father's hands would crack down on his naked back. His trousers were worn through at the knees from the innumerable times he had crouched in front of the home altar, hoping that God would hear his prayers. But He never did.

His father had beaten him ever since he could remember. He was supposed to pray every hour of every day, and every hour the whip flayed his back. Now and then, a club replaced the whip, and as he grew older, his father used a cat-o'-nine-tails, in which each "tail" was equipped with a tiny metallic spike. By then his back was strewn with scars, and his skin had long since turned numb. It was a good thing that the scar tissue was thicker now than the tender skin of a young boy. The scars didn't break open so easily, and it took longer before they started bleeding.

One time he fell over because his sore knees couldn't hold him up any longer. His father had grabbed a huge club covered with iron nails and whacked the boy's left leg so relentlessly that he had limped ever since. His father must have felt sorry, because after the limp developed, he stopped using the club—or maybe it was only because his son could no longer help in the fields. But the abuse continued, and still God didn't answer his desperate pleas for a better life. Finally, when he was fifteen, deliverance came—not through God but through the plague, which terminated his old father's sadistic life in just three days. Now he was truly alone; his mother had died in childbirth, leaving him at the mercy of his brutal father.

Having never known love and with nobody to comfort him in his fear and desperation, he had begun exacting revenge at a young age. If he couldn't punish God for his birth into such a miserable life, at least he could take vengeance on God's creatures. Why not try and see whether the dear Lord would have mercy and save just one victim from his actions? But it never happened.

He started out killing small birds. He remembered his first sparrow with particular fondness. It was winter when he'd lured it, with a handful of grains, inside the house, where he grasped the bird and twisted its little neck without flinching even one bit. He pulled so fiercely that he tore off the sparrow's head. As he stood there, the bird's head in one hand and the tiny, lifeless body in the other, he felt a tremendous sense of power. For once, he was in control. Quite literally his hands ruled over life and death.

A number of birds followed, but eventually the sensation of power waned, and he began to tackle larger animals. A cat fell for his tricks, and he tortured it for several days before finally killing it. He waited for God to save the creature, but again God didn't interfere. God let him go about his evil deeds. Maybe this was his calling.

The reason he had suffered so much was to make others suffer. That thought eased his pain.

He began to think that God was with him all the time after all, that it was precisely God's will for him to become a strong, hard-edged warrior—someone who was forever free from pain and would retreat from nothing. He prayed regularly and took to flagellating himself until he firmly believed that he was strong enough to be God's chosen warrior.

V.

Present

Anna was already waiting outside the little house next to the Zollturm, where she lived in an apartment on the upper floor.

"What are you doing out here in the cold?" Emily asked.

"I felt cooped up and needed some fresh air," Anna replied. "Don't give me that look! I won't die of cold air."

At least her green eyes sparkle with mischief again, Emily thought, and she took Anna's arm. Laughing, the two friends walked south on Rheinstraße to Schlossstraße, where they stopped in a small corner café and chatted away. The time passed quickly; it was as if nothing had changed.

How funny that Anna's sadness seemed to have vanished almost entirely, Emily thought, as she listened to her friend tell her how, a few days earlier, she had gone for a walk along the Rhine and had almost fallen asleep on one of the benches at the promenade.

"Honestly, my bones were so stiff when I first stood up that I felt like I was walking barefoot on a bed of nails. Suddenly there was this man standing right in front of me. I got really scared, of course—I thought he was going to mug me then and there! But he just smiled and asked me very formally whether he could accompany me home, given the very late hour. He actually called me 'fair lady' or something like that. At first I thought he was totally nuts—I wanted to get away from him as fast as possible. But he looked so serious and thoughtful that I simply couldn't bring myself to refuse."

"I see," Emily smirked. "And what's the name of your new crush?"

Anna blushed. "No, he's not taking Martin's place. He was just nice, that's all."

"Come on, Anna. Why don't you at least admit that he was your type? What did he look like?"

"OK, he *was* attractive. Actually, I couldn't see much of his face. It was quite dark out and snowing madly, and he was wearing a hood. All I saw was that he had brown eyes and blond hair and that he was very tall."

Emily nodded slowly and kept smirking at Anna, whose mouth kept threatening to break out into a grin, and then both of them burst into laughter. Emily was sure Anna was falling for this guy, given how deeply she blushed when Emily pressed her for more information. Emily was elated. At last Anna had taken her mind off that jerk Martin, who had never been worth all that sadness in the first place.

"How's the job?" Emily asked. "How's your fight for the filthy rich coming along?"

Oh, now she's mocking me again, Anna thought. She was well aware of her friend's distaste for everything involving money or capitalism in general. But Anna couldn't help it; she was a financier through and through. And after all, Emily wasn't complaining about the profits she had gained thanks to Anna's investment tips. It wasn't really the money itself that attracted Anna to banking. She simply loved the things she'd be able to do with the money someday. Like moving to an actual house and owning her own garden. She loved flowers, and it was her big dream to plant them on several acres of land, a patch of earth that belonged solely to her and where she was at home. She was doing well at her job as investment advisor with a major bank in Düsseldorf. Soon enough, she'd have enough savings put aside to make her house-and-garden dreams come true.

"Well, the job's stressful, you know that very well. Good for you that you're pursuing a second degree, so you can enjoy life a while longer without any restraints or obligations," she teased.

Emily changed the subject. She knew that Anna was a loveable and loving person. Her friend was simply more pragmatic than she was, tackling her goals with determination. "Now listen," Emily said. "I told you about my feature series. I really need a few more documents from the county archive, and I wanted to ask you if you'd like to come with me. I could really use your help."

But Anna wasn't listening. She had jumped halfway off her seat and was gaping out the window. "Emily, I'm pretty sure I just saw Christopher walk by!"

"Nonsense. That's not even possible," Emily snapped. The sudden change of subject disappointed her. The last thing she wanted was to rehash that story for the gazillionth time. Not today. Not now.

"You know that they are both in Berlin. Why should Christopher return alone and then take a walk through Zons? That doesn't make sense. You must have confused him with someone else."

"Well, maybe I did," Anna said, not so sure anymore about what she'd seen. She shrugged. "I could have sworn it was him. But you have a point there: it wouldn't make any sense. I was probably wrong. Maybe my nerves. Rationally, I'm over this unbelievable thing between Martin and Christopher, but maybe my subconscious hasn't let go yet and is playing tricks on me." She sat down again. "You were just about to ask me something. Right, the county archive. Of course I'm coming with you. Let's go right now!"

She got up and left some money on the table. "My treat, you poor student!"

.   .   .

Half an hour later they stood inside the county archive. The air smelled terribly stuffy and the walls were covered with a grayish layer of dirt. Here and there the old wallpaper was peeling off. The figure that came limping toward them from one of the back rooms fit perfectly in the general setting. The archivist had thinning, gray hair; the horn-rimmed glasses on his nose were so huge they almost covered his entire face. His dull, dark eyes peered, bug-like, at Anna and Emily.

"How may I help you ladies?" Attempting a smile, his face contorted into a grimace, and the two friends could see that he was missing at least one of his front teeth.

"We're looking for documents concerning the Zons murder cases from 1495."

"I take it you're looking for the so-called puzzle killer?"

Without giving them another look, he turned around and limped back to a room in the rear. A rustling sound suggested that he was rummaging through heaps of paperwork. Anna and Emily exchanged glances.

"I'm really glad you came with me," Emily said under her breath.

"Me too. This place is eerie," Anna whispered in Emily's ear.

Before long, the weird archivist returned, his arms laden with overstuffed files that he deposited on the table in front of Anna and Emily.

"Let me see," he grumbled. "Ah, here we go. These are Bastian Mühlenberg's personal notes, and here we also have the records of the doctor who was part of the murder investigations. There are more accounts from a later date. Josef Hugo's commentary could be of interest to you. He was a lay assessor in Zons, but that was around 1760. Probably too late for the puzzle killer. In any event, you will have to research who wrote what about those cases. What a tragedy for our small, peaceful Zons back then! To think that an infamous killer from Cologne managed to bust out of the Juddeturm just to continue his murderous deeds in Zons."

VI.
Five Hundred Years Ago

The chains cut deep into his wrists. But to a Lord's Warrior, pain was an honor.

He had not been careful enough. That sweet little blonde had befuddled him with all her innocence and fear. Her body's beautiful aroma had been more enticing than that of the other young girls. Even now the thought of her sent marvelous chills up and down his spine.

At the memory of her tender, milky-white skin and the fantastic final moment when the light disappeared forever from her eyes, feelings of arousal stirred in his groin. And yet, that little tart had deserved her death. He'd had to punish her. She had bewildered him in such a beguiling way that he'd ended up caught by the Cologne City Guard. In his ecstasy he hadn't gagged her thoroughly enough, and she'd let out a last, loud scream.

He could have run, but he'd wanted to savor that last moment. When they caught him, he was still inside her. The City Guard soldiers took one look at the young girl who had been brutally tortured and raped, and they vomited. He would have preferred to exhibit her by hanging her on the closest tree so that everyone could see her. But it was too late for that now.

Roaring and yelling, they had wrestled him down. One of the men had to be the blonde's father, because he was the most brutal of them all, and he never stopped crying.

He reveled in his pain and the excitement around him here, but now they wanted to transfer him from Cologne to Neuss, where he would likely be executed.

Gagged and fettered, he had been put on the bed of a jostling cart. They'd been traveling through the frigid cold for hours, and by now he was so thoroughly chilled to the bones that he had lost even the slightest sensation in his limbs. But at least now he couldn't feel his damaged leg anymore, either. The little blonde's father had battered his left leg—the one that was stiff anyway—so thoroughly that his limping had worsened as a consequence.

Two mounted soldiers patrolled at the side of the cart; with effort, he managed to overhear some of their conversation. If he'd heard right, they wanted to halt in Zons for a last break and lock him up in the *Juddeturm* for the night. He knew about that Juddeturm in Zons. That's where they chained the prisoners and lowered them down into a dungeon thirty-six feet deep. The walls were more than six feet thick, and the only way out was through a small iron grating on the ceiling, which also served as the only source of light. Meals were lowered down through the same grating, attached to a rope on a winch. He'd never heard of anyone who had managed to escape. Only if they put him in one of the upper cells did he have even a chance to break out—but he was sure that, with God at his side, he would find a way to flee.

And, indeed, God was with him. The infamous dungeon was already overcrowded; they locked him in a cell on one of the upper levels, just as he had hoped.

21

Fantastic, he thought. Here, he could even catch a little blast of heat emanating from the small oven that was supposed to warm the castle soldiers.

He had heard quite a bit about Zons from an old psychic. The trapezoid-shaped layout of the city wall had always interested him. The fortified wall had been built with basaltic rocks; it ran about 1,000 feet from north to south and about 820 feet from west to east. At each corner of the city wall was a different tower: in the northeast, the rectangular Zollturm. In the northwest was the round Krötschenturm; in the southwest, the Mühlenturm or Miller's Tower, also round; and in the southeast, the Schlossturm, the Castle Tower. The round Juddeturm was located within the walls, next to Burg Friedestrom, the castle.

According to what the old psychic had once told him, a secret corridor linked the Juddeturm with the castle. The old man had told him that on clear nights during a full moon, the corner points of the town exactly mirrored the corner points of a famous constellation. On those nights, legend had it, if you stood on top of one particular tower, you'd be standing directly under a magic star in the constellation and could, through God's divine light, absorb strength and power.

He had heard those stories a long time ago, when he was still a young boy. The psychic was the only person he could recall from his childhood who had treated him somewhat kindly. Granted, he only saw the old man once a month; the man was also a juggler, and he would come to town with his fellow circus people and set up camp on the marketplace in Cologne, close to his father's farm. Still, it was the only affection he had ever known. The old man sought him out after the performances, showed him the stars and taught him how to use them for orientation. He had told the boy that the small town of Zons had a special connection with the heavenly bodies.

Now that boy had grown up, and he knew exactly what to do once he managed to break free.

.   .   .

1 6 K 1 7 M 1 8 Z. He carved those six magic numbers and three letters into the thick wood of the door. Two numbers were missing—a *9* and another *1*, as well as the final letter—but just as he was about to carve the last two numbers, the sharp knife blade, which he'd successfully smuggled into the Juddeturm, broke on the hard wood. No matter—at least he had been able to carve the most important symbols. Plus, he was satisfied with the inverted balance in the series of numbers and letters. It was quite masterfully done, actually. Nobody would ever crack this code except, perhaps, the old psychic. These were his magic symbols, showing him the path to divine power. He was extremely gratified with himself and the world.

VII.
Present

The two hot babes left his archive shortly after they borrowed the massive files. He wished they had stayed a little longer. He would gladly have filled them in on every detail of the historic murder cases. But he had sensed the girls' uneasiness and how they'd wanted to get away from this place—his second home for thirty years—as fast as possible.

The pretty brunette with her shining, intelligent eyes had shown particular interest in the case. He, in turn, would have enjoyed demonstrating his particular interest in her: running the tip of his tongue down her slender, white neck while grabbing her long hair and pulling her head back. At just the thought, a wave of excitement coursed through his veins.

All those pretty young girls out there in the world—they would never recognize in him the man he truly was! All they saw was a limping, ugly old man, when in fact there was much more to him that made him someone special. Did the brown-haired beauty, for instance, realize that he knew every detail of the medieval history of Zons?

At least he'd garnered more respect and attention from the young man who'd come, several months ago, professing interest in the historic murder cases. That fellow had talked with him for many hours, and the archivist got to show just how smart he was; he knew the answer to each and every question. Well, who knew; maybe the two beauties would return with a bunch of questions. In any event, deep in his heart he hoped that the brunette, the one with the most apparent interest in the cases, would come back and fix her knowing gaze on his face, drinking in every word of his knowledge. He could wait.

.   .   .

"Oh my God, Emily, the way that guy stared at you? That was really creepy. Do me a favor and don't go back there by yourself. At least not when he's on duty!"

"I know, he was totally creepy. And it smelled so horrible in the archives. Who knows what kind of stuff that weirdo is hiding in those back rooms."

As they approached Anna's apartment at Rheinstraße 4, the two friends could see their breath in the bone-chilling air. Although it was only early December, temperatures had already dropped below freezing. Maybe this would be one of those rare years with a white Christmas. Shivering and with shoulders hunched against the cold, Anna and Emily ran the remaining distance and felt relief when they finally stepped inside Anna's warm apartment.

Anna made hot tea, and the two friends sank onto opposite corners of the couch, where they went through the documents that they'd spread out in front of them. According to the files, the killer was one Dietrich Hellenbroich of Cologne. He had grown up on a farm at the northern end of Cologne. His mother had died in childbirth, and his father raised him alone until he fell victim to a

25

huge plague pandemic when Dietrich was only fifteen. Dietrich had inherited the paternal farm—and shortly thereafter, girls from the vicinity began to disappear.

Neighbors suspected Dietrich, but no evidence was brought against him, and for ten years he lived undisturbed on his property—until November 1495. He was caught in the very act of brutally raping and slowly strangling the chief castle guard's youngest daughter. The girl must have defended herself fiercely and screamed loudly for the guards. While they arrived too late for her rescue, they were in time to capture Hellenbroich, the gruesome killer.

Because the girl's family originally hailed from Neuss, her father was adamant that the killer be transferred to Neuss for his execution. He wanted a public execution under the eyes of all of his daughter's loved ones and friends. It was the only act of revenge he could offer his murdered child.

The public execution never happened. Dietrich Hellenbroich had managed to escape during his transfer from Cologne to Neuss, and the Zons city guards' negligence was to blame. At the time, more modern locks were being tested for the cells in the Juddeturm, and somehow, the killer had been able to smuggle a knife blade with him—which allowed him to break out of the heavily guarded tower in the early-morning hours of December 15, 1495. He escaped unnoticed through a secret corridor that linked the tower with the castle. How he knew about or discovered the secret corridor remained a mystery. Only one thing was known for sure: on the day of his release he preyed on yet another victim, the first of the Zons victims: young Elisabeth Kreuzer. That was when Bastian Mühlenberg took over the investigations.

VIII.
Five Hundred Years Ago

Including a physician in the inspection of a body was not yet a common practice, but Bastian had a gut feeling that he might gain more helpful insights if he did. So that same night they carried Elisabeth Kreuzer's body to the only doctor residing in Zons.

The previous day, really everything had gone wrong. As if it weren't enough that Dietrich Hellenbroich, the Cologne killer, had managed to escaped from the Juddeturm, he was still at large, despite Zons being the kind of small town where everyone knew each other and it seemed impossible to hide. And yet no sooner had Hellenbroich made his escape than young Elisabeth Kreuzer had tragically crossed his path.

Bastian knew that Elisabeth's mother suffered from pneumonia and that Elisabeth had been asked to stay home all day and take care of her three young siblings. For some reason, however, she must have left the house. How else would she have run into Dietrich Hellenbroich?

Even his torchlight and last night's full moon had not been sufficient to get a detailed overview of the lesions on Elisabeth's body,

so Bastian had arranged to meet up with the doctor again at daybreak. Together they would look for possible clues.

The bastard had to be hiding somewhere. For the remainder of
the night, Bastian was chasing sleep, never finding a moment's rest.
He was almost relieved when the first rays of sunlight poked through
the window. He quickly ate his oatmeal and walked directly to the
local doctor's house. Josef Hesemann lived on Grünwaldstraße, less
than five minutes away. Josef hadn't slept a wink last night either
and looked bone tired.

Never in the doctor's career had he been faced with such a
gruesome, disturbing sight. He had known bubbly and endearing
Elisabeth for many years, but now he had trouble recognizing her as
the debased and bruised body in front of him.

He had laid her out in his small, enclosed inner courtyard. In
broad daylight they wouldn't need candles or torches. Carefully,
Josef removed her clothing. At first Bastian looked away, embarrassed, but Josef said, "Bastian, you need to take a look in order to
find traces the murderer left behind. I don't think Elisabeth would
mind you looking . . . given the circumstances." So Bastian braced
himself and looked down at Elisabeth's body.

Her skin was as white as if a demon had sucked every last drop
of blood out of her veins. In between her thighs, however, the skin
had turned blue, and Bastian could see that her wrists and ankles
were red and abraded.

"She was probably still alive when he fettered her," Josef told
Bastian, "but probably dead when he suspended her on that chain.
Otherwise, her right wrist would be much more swollen. I'm pretty
sure that at that point her heart had stopped pumping blood. He
must have strangled her beforehand."

Josef then opened Elisabeth's mouth and stuck his nose inside.
He noticed a strong smell of fermented wine.

"Shortly before her death she must have had quite a bit of wine. I pray she was so drunk that she had already passed out when he raped her," Josef said, wincing slightly as he cast another glance between her thighs. There were clear signs of sexual assault.

The two men washed the body with a damp cloth, working quietly and carefully. Now they could see numerous scratch marks all over her skin. All of her hair had been shaved, and her scalp was covered with coagulated and crusted blood, which required some effort on Bastian's part to clean.

"It's odd, but I would say he cut something into her scalp, something almost like symbols. Look here, Josef!" Bastian whispered hoarsely, unable to restrain his excitement at finding a possible clue.

He recognized a *1*, a *6*, and the letter *K*. What could that mean?

"Could be the killer's initials?" Josef suggested.

"No, the demon's name is Dietrich Hellenbroich. No letter *K* in that name," Bastian muttered.

He searched for his notebook and wrote down the numbers and letters. Strange. What if *K* stood for *Köln*, the German spelling of Cologne? But that didn't explain the numbers. No matter how hard they tried, they couldn't wrap their heads around it.

While Josef was dressing the body again, some pebbles trickled to the ground.

"Look here, Bastian, I hadn't seen those earlier," Josef said. "They must have been inside the hem of her skirts." Josef frowned at Bastian.

Bastian collected the pebbles while Josef continued to examine Elisabeth's clothes more thoroughly.

"The blood alone can't be the only reason her clothes are still damp," the doctor said. "Can you recall whether her clothes were wet when you found her last night?"

Bastian tried to recall the previous night's events. The sight of Elisabeth had profoundly shocked him. In his head, he went through every single detail.

"I think at least a part of her gown was wet," he answered finally. "Actually, I'm pretty certain about that."

Josef nodded slowly and spoke as if he was trying to track down a memory.

"I'd say she was in the Rhine. Just last week, my little one, Agnes, was collecting stones at the river banks, and they look just the same as these." With those words he went inside the house and returned, a small basket in one hand.

"Father, what are you doing with my stones?" a little girl shouted excitedly and came running into the yard. Bastian managed to throw a large linen sheet over the dead body, sparing the girl the sight of poor Elisabeth.

"Agnes, don't you come out here! Go back inside, now! You know you are not supposed to come out to the yard!"

The small girl's face turned deep red. She stamped her feet, turned around, and ran back inside, sulking ostentatiously.

"See for yourself, Bastian, the pebbles are identical," Josef repeated, holding a few of the pebbles from Elisabeth's clothes in his right hand and a few from the basket in his left hand.

From his own experience Bastian understood immediately what Josef was talking about. He had walked along the Rhine often enough to know that not all pebbles were alike. Some of them were merely exposed to the running water, but others—like the ones Josef held in his hands—bore striated marks from being jammed against wooden posts. They could originate from only one place: the Rhine pier in Zons.

"We should examine the pier immediately. He could still be hiding nearby!" Bastian jumped to his feet.

"Let me go get Wernhart and we're off. He can help us with the search. Six eyes see more than four. Besides, Wernhart is burly and strong. Just in case we find that monster!"

.   .   .

For half a day they had searched the riverbanks and the surrounding flood plain of the Rhine, in the biting cold and against a relentlessly blowing wind. Starting out at the pier where they believed the pebbles came from, they had marched three miles upriver and another three miles downriver, thoroughly sussing out every possible hiding place. In the end, they hadn't found a trace of the killer, not a single one. Wernhart claimed he discovered several footprints, but those could have been from anyone.

Thoroughly chilled and exhausted, the three men stopped by a tavern in Zons and sat down, each looking somber and disappointed. They had found no trace of Dietrich Hellenbroich and his ghastly deeds, and they were no closer to understanding why Elisabeth, of all people, had fallen into his hands or why he had carved an inscrutable series of symbols into her scalp.

The only thing Bastian knew was that the killer had left his Cologne victim's hair untouched. Bastian had thoroughly questioned his colleagues from the Cologne City Guard, and he was sure that the soldiers would have remembered a detail as conspicuous as a shaved scalp. He racked his brains wondering what he might have overlooked.

His companions wanted to order another round of mead, but Bastian waved them off.

"I'm sated and warm," he said, standing up. The inexplicable scalp carvings made him keen to go over everything Hellenbroich had touched. "I'm running over to the Juddeturm to take another look at Hellenbroich's cell." He grabbed his gown and left the tavern.

At the Juddeturm, he took the stairs that led to the upper floor and opened the heavy wooden door of the cell.

He looked around. It reeked of urine and sweat, but there was not much to be seen. A thin layer of hay occupied one corner of the room. In another corner, a piece of bread sitting next to a water jar had gone stale and moldy. Otherwise the cell was completely empty.

The day before, they had found a broken knife blade on the threshold, their only lead. Bastian let out a long sigh. Just as he was about to step out the door, he noticed, from the corner of his eye, some irregularities in the surface of the wood.

"Well, well," he murmured.

Finally he had discovered something. There were signs carved into the wooden door. He immediately recognized the first two numbers and one of the letters. They were identical to the ones on Elisabeth's scalp. The carvings were clearly the first pieces of a puzzle—but would he be able to solve it? He ran his fingertips over the deeply gouged marks in the wooden door.

"You sick, sick man, what were you thinking?" he muttered.

.   .   .

A week ago they had been searching for him. He had watched as they'd stomped up and down the banks of the Rhine for hours, sometimes examining handfuls of pebbles. For some reason they hadn't considered entering the poor farmer's hut that they passed. Well, they had knocked outside and pressed the man with questions, but they never noticed that Hellenbroich was pressing a knife against the farmer's back. Good man, he carried it off very well and answered all their questions without betraying him.

He must admit, he was stunned when he realized that they had found the exact spot where he'd attacked his first Zons victim. That girl was so sweet and so wonderfully tipsy from all the red wine he'd forced down her gullet, after he had beat her with a stone until she fell unconscious. Usually he liked it when they fought back, but this time was different. This girl was the first part of an artwork that he would dedicate to God, his master—the first piece of a puzzle in which only he had control over the missing pieces. Soon enough he would both capture and create his second sweet and lovely piece.

He limped to the window of the small farmhouse and looked for a long time toward Zons. The girl's fresh and wholesome perfume seemed to waft in through the drafty window with the breeze. The thought raised the thin hair on his forearms and made his eyes gleam.

. . .

For the past three weeks, Bastian had been going through his notes over and over again. He turned page after page, recalled every minute detail. He could sense with almost physical certainty that Hellenbroich was still in town. Elisabeth's killing had been premeditated, planned and executed in cold blood. The killer knew exactly what he was after. And Bastian knew that the gruesome code carved in the girl's scalp and echoed on the cell door in the Juddeturm were obviously linked.

It was also clear to Bastian that the killer *wanted* him to follow his tracks, that he enjoyed being chased, always staying one step ahead. Bastian had the sad premonition that Elisabeth would not be Hellenbroich's last victim. Yet he also knew that deciphering the code might be the first step in forestalling another murder.

Granted, they had bolstered up the City Guard's staff, and there were control posts now at each of the main gates, scrutinizing everyone who entered or left the city, but almost four weeks had passed since the murder and everyone thought that Dietrich Hellenbroich was long gone. Bastian, however, was obsessed; he simply couldn't let this whole affair go. He had sent guards to Cologne to find out more about the killer and his farm. Though they'd come back empty-handed, Bastian's worrisome premonition persisted.

Worse, Bastian felt that he stood pretty much alone with his presentiment of danger. Not even Josef Hesemann, the doctor, would listen to him any longer. As a matter of fact, just the day before, Hesemann had urged Bastian to drink a goblet of wine before going to bed in order to relax his nerves.

But he simply knew that the killer was still close. Tomorrow in the early morning he would depart for Cologne and take a look for himself at the killer's farm. Maybe he would find clues about Hellenbroich's next steps, and if he was lucky he could stop him before yet another young girl lost her life.

IX.
Present

Anna walked along the bank of the Rhine. It was a clear, bright day; the sunshine sparkled on the water. Cheerfully daydreaming, her thoughts wandered freely until, suddenly, she noticed someone squatting ahead in the distance. The silhouette seemed somehow familiar. Curious, she quickened her pace and approached the person.

He had his back to her, so she could discern only his broad shoulders and his wind-blown blond hair. Even so, she knew immediately who he was. She recalled the evening two weeks ago when he had walked her home in the thick of a snowstorm.

All of a sudden he turned around as if he had felt her glance on his back. His dark brown eyes smiled at her. She felt her knees getting weak and desperately tried to think of something to say. Not a single word came to mind. All she managed was a stiff, short nod. Fortunately, he eased the situation.

"Hello, my lady, how are you? I am glad to see you again."

Just as she was about to reply, he literally vanished. Bastian was gone. And that was not all: the Rhine also faded away until it disappeared and Anna found herself standing alone in the dark. Startled, she opened her eyes and sat up. It was nine o'clock at night. She had fallen asleep on her sofa.

Her throat felt dry. Slowly she got to her feet and, still half-asleep, walked over to the kitchen. She took a water glass off the shelf, and while water ran from the faucet she glanced down onto the street. Strange. Someone was standing under the streetlamp and looking up to her window.

At first she worried that it was a stalker, but when she took a closer look, she thought she recognized the man she had just been dreaming of. Indeed, he was waving at her. Now she was convinced that it had to be that Bastian guy. Wait, was that really his name or had she only dreamt it? She waved back at him, took a big gulp of water, shrugged off her rumpled work clothes, and hurried into jeans and a sweater. She tiptoed down the stairs and quietly opened the door.

"Hello there, can I help you?" she whispered.

"No, thank you. I just wanted to check on you, to make sure everything is good with you."

"Well, thank you. I'm doing fine," Anna replied. After a short moment of silence, she ventured, "Would you like to join me for a cup of tea?"

"With pleasure—if you don't mind letting a stranger into your apartment at such a late hour."

Anna opened the door a bit wider and waved him inside. In fact, her audacity at inviting a complete stranger into her apartment scared her a little bit, but her gut feeling told her she was safe with him. He followed her up the stairs, and she motioned him to take a seat at the kitchen table.

"It was very kind of you to walk me home the other night," Anna said while heating water for their tea. "Truly, it was quite late, snowing like mad, and pitch-dark." She paused.

"By the way, my name is Anna."

"Pleased to meet you. I'm Bastian," he replied, not registering Anna's look of surprise. "I just wanted to make sure nothing happened to you. I often check in here to make sure that everything is fine."

"Oh, I see—so you must belong to that new civil watch squad that took up duty here in Zons last month? I actually thought the mayor wasn't that serious about it. Well, at least that's what the media made me think. They were always mocking the initiative because you never really see anyone." Anna chatted breathlessly and didn't even wait for Bastian's answer; she took his brief nod as a confirmation and kept chattering on, engaging him in a cheerful conversation about all the things that made Zons so special.

"Have you been living here a long time?" she asked him.

"Oh, yes. For a very long time. Sometimes it even seems much too long for my taste." He smiled at her.

The conversation was pleasant, and an hour had passed easily when he suggested that, given the late hour, he should leave so Anna could get ready for bed. At first Anna felt a slight disappointment, but she knew it was the right thing to do.

When he said good-bye, he placed a gentle kiss on the back of her hand. His old-fashioned mannerisms and speech struck Anna as somewhat odd but also attractive in a peculiar way. Martin had never treated her with any chivalry—or even the attentiveness one would expect of a boyfriend—and she was so charmed by Bastian's quaint ways that she completely forgot to ask for his phone number. When she realized that he hadn't asked for hers, either, she felt another little sting of disappointment. But since she didn't want to spoil her blissful mood, she decided to cherish their nice encounter until the next one, which, she strongly hoped, would happen soon.

In the middle of the night Anna opened her eyes. Had the conversation with Bastian been real or part of that same vivid dream? Suddenly she wasn't sure anymore whether Bastian had really sat in her apartment and gently kissed her hand good-bye, or whether it had been just another dream.

.   .   .

Oliver Bergmann admired himself in the mirror. His new uniform suited him extraordinarily well. It was official: as recently as last week he had been promoted and now belonged to the Crime Commission of the police department in Neuss, Rhine County. His jurisdiction included Zons, and he was in charge of violent offenses—murder, rape, robbery, physical assault, and poisoning.

Almost a thousand of these offenses were committed annually. With a crime-clearance rate hovering around 80 percent, Bergmann's team was one of the most successful in the entire county police.

A lucky coincidence had triggered his rapid promotion into the prestigious Crime Commission. Just a few months ago he had still been a regular patrolman who issued traffic citations and followed up on complaints about noise nuisance. Yet he had been the pivotal assistant to his colleagues who were trying to solve the murder of a homeless man at the Neuss Central Station. He had pulled out his cell phone at the right moment and filmed the perpetrator on the run. It had already been dark, but the police technicians nevertheless managed to use his cell-phone video to isolate the license plate of the killer's car, making it possible to catch the guy swiftly. Chief of Detectives Hans Steuermark had been so impressed with Bergmann's instincts and quick actions that he soon invited Bergmann to join his team, even though the patrolman's final grades from the Academy hadn't been the best. But Steuermark couldn't care less. He'd rejected candidates with better grades; he wasn't one to put a high price on theoretical knowledge displayed and praised on paper. He relied on promptness, logical thinking, and the right gut instinct.

The phone rang, and when Oliver saw the number on the display he frowned. His mother again. It was only eight o'clock in the morning, and this was her second call. Since Oliver's father had passed away the year before, his mother felt lonely in the big house. Oliver visited her as often as he could and spoke almost daily with her on the phone. They generally had a good relationship, but she was starting to get on his nerves. He could already surmise what she wanted to ask him. He had announced his visit for the weekend, and now she was probably fussing about the dinner menu. Just a moment ago she had called to ask whether she should also invite his cousin over, and Oliver couldn't think of anything else for her to ask about now but the food.

"HI, Mom," he said. "What's up?"

And, indeed, she asked him what he wanted her to cook on the weekend. Since he had to report for duty at the precinct in fifteen minutes, he cut it short and headed out.

It took him less than ten minutes to arrive at his office, where his partner Klaus already awaited him.

"Oliver, we have to leave right away. Steuermark wants us to take on the Body in the Woods case. The guys from Düsseldorf are already on-site, and I really don't want them to snatch another case from us."

Oliver thought about Klaus's previous case. Oliver hadn't been on board yet, but he knew that Klaus had been investigating the murder of a seven-year-old girl for almost a year, and that since Klaus wasn't the fastest detective, the Düsseldorf homicide division had ended up taking over the entire case. It had been a real comedown for Klaus after pouring a lot of time and work into the investigations—and, as it turned out, he had been on the right track. But the guys from the state capital had been pressing hard because the girl was from a notable local family, and they wanted the case solved as quickly as possible.

Klaus made a point of playing it safe when investigating. He wouldn't make an accusation until he was absolutely certain. But in the case of the young girl, there had been pressure to come up with a suspect at any cost, and when they finally arrested someone, they were only 80 percent sure it was the right guy. Since then Klaus had taken to speeding up his investigations; today he didn't even give Oliver time to grab a coffee.

They drove to a patch of forest adjacent to the Autobahn A57 near Neuss. A lumberjack had discovered the body of a man in his late twenties, fully dressed except for his shoes, which were missing. There was no wallet on him. And the killer had burned the man's fingertips, probably in order to prevent a fast identification of the victim.

Thanks to witness statements and an analysis of the tire marks, they had so far been able to determine that the killer must have driven a Ford. Two weeks ago, a wallet had been found in a household garbage can not far from a large housing complex in Düsseldorf; the information on the ID card matched the details of a young man who'd been reported missing eight weeks earlier. As far as Oliver was concerned, identification of the body should be imminent.

X.

Five Hundred Years Ago

Bastian was impressed when he saw Dietrich Hellenbroich's property. The farm was huge, with two large barns, numerous stables, a main house, and three smaller buildings for the employees, all grouped around a big inner yard. The premises appeared to be well kept, despite Hellenbroich's prolonged absence of several weeks. Just as Bastian was wondering who was operating the farm in the murderer's absence, a sturdy old man stepped out of one of the stables, as if anticipating Bastian's question.

"Hail, stranger," said the old man. "What can I do for you?"

Bastian quickly appraised the man: he was in very good physical shape for his age, but he was totally blind. His eyes were clouded over, almost completely white. Only a soft, dark shadow hinted that the old man's eyes must once have been brown. His long hair was thick and full, entirely gray, as were his bushy eyebrows. As he stood there with his hair blowing in the wind and those blind eyes, a long wooden cane in his right hand, he reminded Bastian of a magician.

Truth be told, Bastian had only seen magicians from a distance. As a boy he'd had to sneak out of his house to catch some forbidden glances of the magic acts at the jugglers' fairs. His mother had been adamant about not letting him go to the fairs; she was convinced that traveling folks were evil, devilish creatures with witches' brews and charms that poisoned and cursed innocent, upright people.

In fact, when he was a boy, Bastian had known of one such unfortunate person. The woman lived nearby in Zons, and rumor had it that a magician's spell had cursed her to remain an old spinster. Indeed, she had lived to a very old age, but not once had a suitor asked her hand in marriage, although in her time she had been considered one of the most beautiful young women in Zons.

His mother had often told him the story of the poor old maid, and as a consequence, Bastian's childhood fascination had gradually evolved into an inexplicable fear of the fairs and the psychics, jugglers, and magicians who peopled them. Bastian reminded himself that the old man standing in front of him now was a farmworker, not a magician; his heart stopped racing, and he returned the friendly greeting.

"My name is Bastian Mühlenberg. I am a member of the City Guard in Zons, and I am looking for the farmer and murderer Dietrich Hellenbroich. During his transfer from Cologne to Neuss he was incarcerated for one night in our Juddeturm, but unfortunately he managed to escape and killed one of our girls. I'm looking for clues. We need to catch him before he has the chance to prey on yet another victim. I hope you can help me and answer some questions."

The old man felt his knees getting weak until they couldn't hold him any longer. With a loud sigh he put down his cane. Covering his whole face with his hands, he sank to the ground, muttering words that Bastian could barely make out.

"Oh no . . . Dietrich. Not Zons. I always said it's a holy city . . . must not be desecrated."

"What does that mean? Zons a holy city?" Bastian stooped to grab the man under his arms and help him into the kitchen of the main house. "Didn't they tell you here that Dietrich Hellenbroich has another notch on his belt—another girl killed?" Bastian asked.

"No. The guards from Cologne searched everything and didn't leave a stone unturned, but they didn't say a single word about a dead girl in Zons." The old man painstakingly lifted a cup to his lips.

"Oh, yech!" He spit out the weak ale. "Marta! I need something stronger. Bring me a chalice of wine. The good one—and another goblet for my young guest here. And hurry up, will you, woman!" The maid looked frightened and scurried off to obey.

"Look," the old man continued with his wine in hand, "Dietrich was a very special boy. Deep down he is a good soul, but his father battered the little angel that used to live in his heart for so long that the angel flew away. Since then, Dietrich carries only the devil inside him, and the devil burns and destroys every little bit of kindness or affection. I'm afraid Dietrich's soul cannot be saved anymore. It has long disappeared. A very long time ago."

The old man cast his blind eyes steadily onto Bastian, and suddenly Bastian had the impression that the man sitting across from him was not blind at all. He tried to wash away his uneasiness with a big gulp of wine. The alcohol went down smoothly, replacing the chill from his long journey with warmth.

"How do you know Dietrich?" he asked the old man.

"I've known him since he was a little boy. He used to sneak into my performances when he was a young lad. You see, I used to be quite a famous clairvoyant. I even had the honor of entertaining some of the country's most prestigious aristocrats with my art. One day, however, I revealed the truth about the wife of one of those important men—and in his rage he had me blinded. Since then I was no longer suited for a juggler's traveling life. I need a stable place where I can find my way around despite my blindness. More than ten years ago, Dietrich asked me to become chief supervisor on

43

his farm, and I accepted with gratitude. I didn't know how a blind man could be of any use to the farm, but things have worked out well."

It's no surprise that Dietrich would hire a blind, old psychic just to scare off the rest of his staff, Bastian thought. *They were all probably terrified that he'd cast a spell on them if they didn't submissively endure the murderer's brutal manner.*

As if the old man had read this thoughts, he pronounced, "Bastian Mühlenberg, you have a pure soul and are full of love. That's why I have decided to tell you a secret I only share with very few people."

"What secret? And what did you mean earlier, when you referred to Zons as a holy city?"

"Oh, that. I can easily let you in on what I know about the holy city of Zons," the old man whispered, leaning in closer to Bastian. His breath was warm and reeked of alcohol, and Bastian tried to overcome his nausea and remain close to his host.

"Dietrich's mother was from there. That's why to him it is a holy city!" The old man laughed out loud and then stood up and rested his hand on Bastian's shoulder.

"Bastian Mühlenberg, bestow me the honor and stay overnight. Tonight is the January full moon, and I would like to show you something." With these words, he abruptly walked out of the parlor and left Bastian alone.

So his first instinct had not betrayed him: Bastian had in fact encountered a real magician—or clairvoyant, or whatever he was—in the flesh. At first glance, he seemed rather sinister. His acquaintance with Dietrich Hellenbroich was suspicious enough. But Bastian couldn't say that the old man had threatened or even cursed him in any way. Should he stay overnight? His mother, God bless her, would turn over in her grave if she knew.

But she didn't know, and Bastian was curious to learn about the secret the magician had mentioned. Of course, it could well be a trap. Would the old man try to kill Bastian in his sleep? Well, he could have done so earlier by putting something into his wine. Bastian had emptied his entire goblet, but all he felt was pleasantly relaxed and drowsy.

No, he thought to himself, *if he really wanted to kill me, he already had a good chance.* Slowly he shook his head.

"I will accept your kind offer. I shall stay overnight."

A few minutes later the maid appeared in the doorway and asked Bastian if she could show him to his room. He followed her to the staff living quarters on the left side of the main house and gratefully sank down on the bed as soon as she had left the room.

·   ·   ·

"Hey, wake up! Time to go!" The old psychic hammered on Bastian's door.

Bastian rubbed his eyes and jumped out of bed. His stomach growled. He noticed that it was dark out. He must have fallen asleep and missed dinner. He opened the door.

The old man offered him some buttered bread, cheese, and a goblet of wine. "Here, eat this. I believe you might need some refreshment," he said. "You slept so profoundly, I didn't want to wake you earlier. But now we have to go, or we'll miss an incredible spectacle tonight."

Gratefully, Bastian devoured the food and wine. His appetite was voracious. The old man patted his back.

"My young fellow, had I known how hungry you were, I would have called you for dinner!"

"How can you tell that I have eaten everything, when you are blind?" Bastian asked, incredulous.

45

"From the way you are smacking your lips. I can tell without seeing that your plate is empty. Hearing is enough." The old man grinned at him. "Come on now. We'll go over to the meadow behind the main house, and I will show you a magic rectangle. Should you still be hungry afterward, there's plenty of bread and wine in the kitchen for you."

With these words he gently pushed Bastian through the door and slipped his arm under Bastian's. They hurried across the inner yard. A small gate led them onto a huge meadow. Four large torches were already set up in the shape of a right-angled trapezoid. Each torch stood about five to seven feet from the next one in the frosty grass.

The night air was frigid, and a thin layer of icy snow covered the meadow, reflecting the light from the full moon. Bastian rubbed his cold hands together and looked over at the old man, who was fishing in the pockets of his gown and finally held up two flint stones and some tinder.

"Strike a spark and light those four torches, please."

Bastian did as he was told. After gnashing the stones together, he produced some sparks, and the tinder began to glow. Then he held a piece of brushwood into the embers and waited until he saw a small flame. He lit the first torch, pulled it out of the ground, lit the remaining three torches with its flame, and then shoved it back into the frozen earth.

"Why do you need light when you can't see anyway? Besides, the full moon is so bright, one hardly needs torches."

"You will see *for* me, Bastian Mühlenberg. Tell me exactly how many feet the torches are apart."

Bastian walked the distance between the first two torches. Six feet. Then he turned in a right angle and walked from the second to the third torch. This time, he measured seven feet. Again he turned left and now measured eight feet. He repeated the left turn and walked back to the first torch. Nine feet.

"Excellent!" The old man clapped his hands gleefully and ordered, "Now, take me to the first torch."

Bastian guided the psychic to the first torch, where the old man requested that Bastian lie down next to him in the meadow.

"What do you see, Bastian Mühlenberg? What do your young eyes perceive?"

Bastian blinked. The torch's bright glow blinded his eyes, and it was hard to concentrate with the icy layer of snow against his back.

"All I see is the fire from the torch. What else should I see?" he asked, shivering.

"Focus. Ignore the fire and let your eyes see through the glow. What do you see in the sky?"

Bastian tried to focus but couldn't see anything, and his eyes started to water from the cold. But just a second later they adjusted to the brightness of the torch, and suddenly he could make out bright pinpoints in the nocturnal sky.

"I see the stars in the sky above me," he told the old man without averting his glance from the heavens.

The old man nodded. "Would you say the brightest star is right above you?"

"Yes. It seems to be right above the torch."

"Very good. Now go lie down next to each of the remaining torches and repeat everything we just did. Always tell me whether the brightest star shines directly above the torch."

Bastian followed the old man's orders, and indeed it seemed again that one star out of the sparkling bounty shone particularly brightly and always right above the torch. In the end he wasn't sure whether what he saw was real or just an optical illusion, because his eyes had to get past the torches' corona of light. In any case, a large, bright star was shining above each torch, and Bastian could now clearly discern a trapezoid with four bright stars as corner points, pinning it against the indigo sky.

"This is my magical quadrangle!" the old man said with a husky voice and turned his blind eyes to Bastian. "Here you have the secret of orientation. Bastian Mühlenberg, never again will you get lost at night, no matter if you're on firm ground or at sea. This quadrangle is always visible during the full moon, and its measurements always correspond to the distances between the torches. When you use these points for orientation, you will always find your way back."

"Interesting," Bastian said without much conviction. He still didn't quite understand what the old man was getting at.

"The walls around Zons," said the old man, "how are they built? Think hard!"

That's when Bastian understood. The city walls in Zons also formed a right-angled trapezoid. The scales fell from his eyes.

"You mean the walls around Zons are built in the same proportion, six to seven to eight to nine?"

"Exactly," the old psychic whispered. "I showed it to Dietrich a very long time ago. He was obsessed with it, especially after he'd found out that his mother was originally from Zons. He often said he wanted to stand high up on one of the towers on the night of a full moon and look up at the brightest star. He thought he'd somehow sense his mother. She died in childbirth, you know, leaving him alone with his brutal father. I answered the boy that nothing is impossible under a full moon when you are sure to bring enough sacrifices."

"You are saying a girl from Zons could be considered such a sacrifice?" Bastian's voice trembled.

"I always tried to bring Dietrich back onto the right track. But it was too late. I'm afraid you're right, Bastian. I believe he killed the girl and then climbed up one of the towers. I truly hope he got what he was longing for, because then you can be certain that he has moved on and won't cause any more harm in your small town."

"But if that's the case, he would have returned home and you would have seen him, don't you think?"

"I don't know," the old man replied quietly. "I really hope you're wrong, Bastian, and that Dietrich has moved on. But I can't say for sure. Dietrich has a very complicated mind."

With these words, the old man slowly stood and motioned Bastian to do the same. By now it was past midnight, and their muscles were stiff from lying so long in the snowy meadow. It took a long time to lead the old man, stiffened from cold, back to the main house. All Bastian wanted was to sleep. He walked directly to his room, where he immediately fell into a profound slumber.

.   .   .

Early the following day, Bastian got ready for the long journey back to Zons. The trip would take half a day. Politely he bid farewell to the old psychic, thanking him for everything the man had shared with him. Bastian still didn't know how, exactly, the magical trapezoid would be of use to him. But in the hopes that Dietrich Hellenbroich would show up to fulfill his crazy delusion, Bastian would add more guards on each of the four towers, especially on full-moon nights. He couldn't imagine that the killer would be so easily trapped—but it was worth a try. Even if Hellenbroich expected Bastian to visit his farm and encounter the old psychic caretaker, would he expect the old man, whom he had taken into his confidence, to share the secret about the star trapezoid with Bastian? But he had shared it, so Bastian decided that he would acquire a detailed map of the city of Zons and, as early as the following night, he would climb each of the towers of Zons and look up into the starry sky.

Bastian again recalled the bloody carvings in Elisabeth's scalp: a *1*, a *6*, and the letter *K*. These were exactly the same three symbols the killer had carved into the wooden door in the Juddeturm. While the old clairvoyant had been able to explain how the numbers *6*, *7*, *8*, and *9* were connected, nothing explained how the letter *K* fit into all this. Nor, for that matter, the number *1*. No, he still couldn't wrap his head around this puzzle, but he mulled it over and over in his mind as he rode straight back to Zons.

.   .   .

She lifted her eyes to the full moon above her, usually a beautiful sight, lush yellow with small dark spots that formed a face if you looked long enough. But Gertrud couldn't enjoy the moon's beauty on this bright, clear winter's night.

She was lashed to the pier, and the Rhine's frigid water washed across her body up to her throat in short, recurring intervals. With every swooshing wave, the river seemed to swallow another little piece of her body. A few times the waves had been even stronger and she had choked on mouthfuls of icy water because she couldn't lift her head.

The moment he'd attacked her, she had known it had to be Dietrich Hellenbroich, the man who had raped and murdered Elisabeth Kreuzer a month ago and caused such a furor in Zons. Everyone, including herself, had believed that he had left Zons long ago and disappeared for good. Besides, she lived directly next to the Mühlenturm and just a few meters away from a large double gate with a drawbridge where the City Guard kept watch around the clock. This was the only point of entry into Zons from the west. When word of Elisabeth's murder had first come out, she took to locking her door with a huge bolt. But she had grown tired of lifting that heavy thing all the time. Bit by bit, Elisabeth's murder faded from her memory and a sense of safety had covered her instinctive fears like a veil. A few weeks after the murder, she'd gradually begun to forget about the safety measures and had left the door to her house open like she used to do.

In broad daylight he sneaked into her house and ambushed her as she was entering the pantry to choose the ingredients for lunch. He chained her hands and shoved a piece of rough cloth so deep into her throat that she thought—hoped—it would choke her before he laid another hand on her body.

He noticed that she was about to suffocate, however, and loosened the gag just enough for her to breathe. Still in the pantry, he shaved off her hair. By then she was certain that she was about to meet the same fate as Elisabeth. Once she had lost all her marvelous blonde curls, he began to gradually pour liters of red wine into her mouth. In the beginning she had to throw up, but each time he hit her brutally and pinched her nostrils together so she had to swallow more. Eventually she lost consciousness, coming to only when she was lying in the cold water of the Rhine.

Another wave smacked its way up to her lips. Desperate, she tried to lift her head again, when suddenly the madman pulled her out of the water. A terrible foreboding came over her. She couldn't move, let alone defend herself. She noticed gratefully that her body was so frozen she hardly felt anything when he brutally penetrated her and reached his orgasm, making disgusting, groaning sounds. The only thing she felt were his hands strangling her as he raped her. Her first reaction was panic, but then she realized that her suffering would be over any second—and so, in the last moments of Gertrud's life, she tried to seek comfort in the fact that very soon, God would welcome her in paradise.

51

XI.

Present

Emily opened her tired eyes to see a shaft of moonlight shining into her room. Out the window the moon seemed almost full. She looked at her watch.

"Damn," she scolded herself. Once again she'd let herself take a small nap, but it had become very late.

It was past midnight. Her deadline was in two days, and she still hadn't finished the first part of her feature series for the *Rheinische Post*. How could she make it? She had hardly managed to work the previous week, when she'd been ill with a terrible flu. Sweating and feverish, she had spent the days in her bedroom sleeping and downing antibiotics. Her swollen sinuses made her head feel enormous and heavy; it had been too hard to think, let alone write.

Today was the first day she felt better. With Christmas only a few days away, the need to finish the article took on more urgency. The editor had advised her that copyediting would take at least a day, so there was no room for further delays. Anna had been very sweet, coming over in the evenings to feed her chicken soup and make her endless cups of hot tea. She had also thoroughly organized

Emily's research material. Now the documents were spread in a circle around the sofa in Emily's living room.

Emily had almost finished describing the first murder. After a few improvements here or there, Anna, too, had been impressed. But the problem was reconstructing the solution to the fatal puzzle. Emily simply didn't comprehend how to link the numbers and letters that Bastian Mühlenberg, the investigator from the City Guard, had written in his notebook, along with other details of the case. To fully understand the riddle, she needed a historic map of Zons, but where could she find such a thing at this hour of the night?

She Googled "Zons" and "historic map" but didn't find what she needed among the results. Another glance at her watch, and she realized it was already one o'clock in the morning. Damn, she'd have to go see that weird, limping guy in the county archive first thing tomorrow. Maybe Anna would have time to come with her, she thought, before fatigue overwhelmed her and she fell into a deep sleep.

.   .   .

It was eight o'clock in the morning. Anna's cell phone was ringing, but she was in a meeting and couldn't pick up.

"Aaargh," Emily muttered and hung up. "Seems I'll have to go by myself."

In half an hour she was in the county archive, breathing in the damp, fetid smell she remembered from her last visit. It wasn't long before the creepy archivist came limping toward her, a triumphant smile on his face.

"Young lady," he said, leaning in toward her and staring at her breasts, "may I be of further assistance concerning the killer and his puzzle?"

"Yes. I need a historic city map in order to put the pieces together." Emily backed off a step to avoid the archivist's bad breath. It was almost unbearable, but she desperately needed that map.

"Well, certainly. Why don't you come with me and I'll make you a copy? But before that, let me show you the original city map. The copies tend to be of poor quality and you might not be able to recognize everything on them."

"Can't I just wait here, up front?" Emily asked hesitantly.

"My dear, don't you worry. I won't leave you alone in the dark archives. I will be at your side at all times; you can count on that!"

He smirked, and she could see the gap where his tooth had been. He offered her his arm, and Emily followed him uneasily.

I hope this isn't a mistake, she thought and, stiffening up, tried to maintain as wide a distance as possible between herself and the archivist.

He led her into one of the rear rooms. The ceiling was low, but the room itself was far larger than she would have guessed. Huge, old, and dusty shelves were standing in ten neatly organized rows to her left and right. Emily tried to see the back of the room, but it was too far away. Here, the air seemed not only stuffy but actually moldy. She didn't even want to imagine how many dead mice or spiders were decaying under the shelves or, even worse, between all the files, records, documents, and books that were stacked up on them. She could see the old archivist's footsteps in the layer of dust that covered the floor: one clear footprint on the right, and a slurred track from the limping leg on the left.

"Wait here one second," he told her. Emily sat down in a small chair at the end of one of the long rows.

The limping archivist disappeared between the shelves and re-emerged a few moments later clutching a huge roll of paper.

"Here it is! The historic city map of Zons from the fifteenth century."

He licked his lips with the tip of his tongue, carefully unfolded the map, and spread it out on the table in front of Emily.

"Well then, let's take a look, shall we?" He leaned forward, inching closer to Emily who, in turn, leaned backward as subtly as possible.

"Here we have the old city wall. Some claim it was rectangular, but that's wrong."

Emily scanned the map. While the walls ran straight, each of the four sides had a different length. The shortest wall was along the southern end of the city. The mill was located on the left side, and Burg Friedestrom sat on the right. The eastern wall was the longest segment of the city fortification, followed by the western and northern sides, the second- and third-longest respectively.

Back then, four large gates offered access to the city. The only one that was still intact was the Zollturm. The Feldtor in the west, the Südtor, and the eastern gate that had been part of Burg Friedestrom didn't exist anymore. In the fifteenth century, those four gates were the only entrances to the city. Zons must have been quite a safe city, Emily reasoned, at least according to the standards of the time.

The old archivist explained to her that the different lengths of the city wall were built in a proportion of six to seven to eight to nine, giving the whole the shape not of a rectangle but, geometrically speaking, of a trapezoid. A right-angled trapezoid, to be precise.

"What does the inverted balance symbol stand for?" Emily asked the archivist. "See, here, at the lower end of the map?"

He frowned and tugged on his glasses. "The inverted balance stands for an inversion." With these words, he turned the map upside down. "See? Now north is south."

"Yes," Emily replied. "But what's the meaning of it?"

"It is presumed that the master builder of Zons laid out the city based on Corvus, the constellation of the Raven. It appeared among the original constellations mentioned on Ptolemy's list. According to Greek mythology, the raven is linked to Apollo's cup. Look, here." The old man unfolded another map, this one showing the constellations.

Running his fingers over the map, he explained, "In the south, the constellation of the Raven is bounded by Hydra, in the east by the Crater, and in the west by Virgo. Due to the conditions set by the course of the Rhine, they couldn't create an exact copy of the Raven when erecting the walls. They had to turn the whole thing by 180 degrees, bringing what's north to the south. That's what the inverted balance at the bottom of the map indicates."

"You really know a lot about it," Emily said, and the queer old man beamed with pride. He crouched even closer toward Emily and continued his lecture.

"According to Greek mythology, Apollo put a cup in the raven's beak and sent him to a fountain so that he could gather water for an offering to Zeus, Apollo's father. The raven, however, didn't return on time because on the way he perched on a fig tree and ate his fill of the juicy figs. In order to avoid punishment, the sly raven captured a water snake once he arrived at the fountain and brought the snake and the full cup back to Apollo. He lied to Apollo, telling him that the snake had barred the way to the fountain, causing his delay. Apollo, however, saw through the lie and banished the raven, the cup, and the water snake from the earth, flinging them into the firmament where they remain fixed forever. Why he would place them next to Virgo is not clear. Explanations abound."

Emily was visibly impressed by the archivist's knowledge. Still beaming with pride, the old man rolled the maps together again, turned around, and walked back into the aisle from which he had retrieved them. Suddenly Emily felt a cold draft, and then, with a loud bang, the door of the room slammed shut. Startled, she looked over her shoulder, but she couldn't see anything—until she suddenly felt the archivist's damp breath on her neck. She twisted around in panic. His wrinkled, bug-like face was just inches away from her own.

"Don't worry, young lady. New visitors have arrived. When this happens, that door tends to slam shut." As he whispered, she could feel drops of his spittle on her ear.

Swiftly, she jumped from her chair and walked to the door. The old man laughed, amused, and continued to ogle her.

"Your copies, your copies!" He held two sheets out to her. Feeling dizzy, Emily stepped forward and stretched out her right hand. He handed her the papers, but before she could move, he had already covered her hand with his. Emily flinched, but her obvious distaste didn't deter the archivist, who smirked lasciviously as she moved toward the door.

"You're welcome to come by any time, should you have further questions."

"Thank you, but I guess I'm fine for now," Emily replied and yanked at the doorknob. Waves of relief washed through her when the door swung open easily. It took only a few steps to reach the exit, and, once in her car, she took a deep breath before she started the engine. She was relieved to have made it out of the bizarre and moldy county archive safe and sound.

Now, with the new material, she should be able to finish her article by tonight. She was confident that over a nice cup of tea in her living room, with her maps and research material spread around her, she would find the solution to the puzzle quite easily.

. . .

Oliver Bergmann's phone rang.

Oh no, not again, he thought, annoyed.

It was probably the two hundredth caller over the past two months, claiming to have seen a Ford at or near the spot where they found the Body in the Woods, and Oliver was getting really tired of this. In actuality, pursuing leads could be very tedious and dull—not the excitement he'd imagined when starting his new post as detective.

He must have watched too many *CSI* and *Law & Order* episodes on television, where something exciting happened every minute and called for heroic action. Instead, he sat at a desk in an office and answered a never-ending stream of boring phone calls, took notes regarding yet another sighting of yet another Ford for which he subsequently would have to vet the license plate. After that, he'd have to trudge from one auto shop to the next, inquire if and when the respective car had last been repaired, and, well . . . cross off the lead. So far, their search had not produced even the slightest hit.

If this continued, he'd soon become a Ford automotive expert. Such was the lot of the youngest team member. His partner Klaus got to question the witnesses—though so far, equally without any exciting results. But that didn't prevent Oliver from imagining Klaus's task as far more interesting, definitely more rewarding than having to deal with that damned getaway car!

Despite intensive police activity, they had not been able to identify the late twenties Body in the Woods. In the beginning they had hoped for a swift ID, given the fact that his features perfectly matched a missing-persons report that had been issued eight weeks earlier. Yet that promising hot trail had gone up in smoke yesterday when the missing young man had finally materialized in a drunk cell in Bochum, with a BAC of .18 percent but alive. Now they were groping in the dark again, with only two somewhat trustworthy witnesses providing info concerning the getaway car. And whether those leads would prove substantial remained to be seen.

Oliver was bored and frustrated at the same time, and it didn't help that his boss, cranky since the "missing person" had turned up in the drunk tank, appeared hourly at Oliver's desk, inquiring about the status of the investigation.

Oliver wondered how easy it was to disappear in Germany. There was not one single missing-persons report that matched the unknown dead man, not even in the slightest. Oliver shook his head in desperation; something told him they were not tackling this the right way.

XII.

Five Hundred Years Ago

Bastian couldn't believe it. He had been gone for less than two days inspecting Hellenbroich's farm in Cologne when, during the one night of his absence, a second murder had taken place. He felt a sense of foreboding when he approached the city gate and half the City Guard's staff ran frantically toward him.

This time the victim was young Gertrud Minkenberg, and it was clear Hellenbroich had his mind set on killing young girls during the full moon. Bastian blamed himself terribly for his late return. Had he traveled to Cologne only a week earlier, he might have been able to prevent the murder. And had he not been gone at all, he would have at least made sure the guards on duty remained on high alert. Yet a two-day absence had been enough for them to relax their vigilance. After all, during the recent weeks nothing had happened, and so they justified their negligence to him. In a rage he cut the guards' extra rations of mead.

Bastian sought solace with the priest, Father Johannes, who immediately tried to calm him by setting a goblet of strong, hot red wine in front of him. As the alcohol's soothing effect set in, Bastian told the clergyman about his excursion to Cologne and his strange encounter with the old psychic. The priest listened carefully and, after a while, unfolded a map of Zons.

"Well then, let's take a look, my dear Bastian," the priest said and asked Bastian to point out the magical trapezoid.

"*Corvus videt virgo,*" the priest whispered. "You understand the meaning of these words, Bastian?"

"Of course," Bastian answered. "You yourself taught me Latin. It means: The raven sees the virgin."

The old priest laughed. "Well, indeed, but don't draw your conclusions too hastily. Look behind the meaning of the words. Tell me, what do the raven and the virgin symbolize?"

Bastian thought hard. He was familiar with ravens, and of course he knew what a virgin was, but he couldn't come up with a link between the two.

He put his head in his hands and moaned, "I'm no good at solving riddles anymore! Those murders are draining every little bit of my energy."

"Don't give up too easily, my son. You can't lose your mind's power so fast—though admittedly, this marvelous red wine is rather strong." Bastian's old teacher grabbed another map and spread it out in front of them. "Look here. Now can you tell me the meaning of those words?" He gave Bastian an encouraging wink.

Bastian took a quick gulp from his goblet and leaned forward. "Oh, how could I not notice earlier? We are dealing with two constellations!" He smacked his forehead and shook his head balefully at the priest. "Seems you're always a few steps ahead of me!"

The priest patted his shoulder with affection.

"Without you," Bastian exclaimed, "I would still be brooding about the trapezoid-shaped layout of our city!"

He realized now that the psychic hadn't revealed everything. He had made Bastian look directly at the constellation of the Raven without pointing out to him what he was really seeing: the constellation was a right-angled trapezoid, just like Zons.

"Well," Bastian continued, "the killer is obsessed with constellations and the power of the full moon. He chose Zons because his mother was from here and because the magician showed him that the shape of our city walls corresponds with the shape of the Raven." He jotted his thoughts down in his notebook while he spoke.

"Father, do you think he is so drawn to the symbolism of the Raven because it is next to Virgo? After all, he preys only on young maidens."

"I can't see how a simple farmer would have attained such astronomy knowledge. Maybe it's mere coincidence. After all, the psychic didn't mention the names of the constellations to you, either."

"I'm not sure I agree with you there, Father. The psychic told me that Dietrich Hellenbroich is obsessed with the stars and believes that magic forces are released by the full moon. That would explain the times of the killings, right?"

"That is true, both happened during a full moon. But I can't see a real pattern yet," the priest ruminated, "unless . . ." He trailed off, suddenly becoming animated and deftly drawing two crosses on the map.

"Take a look, Bastian. These spots mark the places where the women's bodies were found."

Bastian looked at the crosses. One was next to the city wall, the other at the banks of the Rhine. Elisabeth Kreuzer had been suspended on one of the towers at the Schlossplatz. With Gertrud Minkenberg, the killer hadn't gone to such lengths, abandoning her corpse in the Rhine. Either there was no pattern, or the killer had been disturbed during Gertrud's murder. The doctor had determined that Elisabeth, too, had first been tortured and raped at the

Rhine before the killer suspended her dead body. Bastian leafed through his notes.

"Look here, these are the numbers and letters I found carved into the door in the Juddeturm," Bastian said, "and these ones were carved into Elisabeth's scalp. He wouldn't make all this effort if there's no meaning behind it."

The priest brooded over the killer's code. Indeed, it looked as if with every new victim, the killer presented yet another little piece of a puzzle. Every dead body completed the picture a little bit more. But how sick would someone have to be to kill young women in order to leave messages or complete a puzzle?

The fireplace in the corner crackled loudly and filled the small room with much welcome heat. Bastian, remembering how frozen he'd felt during his trip to Cologne, rubbed his palms against each other and stared into the dancing flames. Suddenly he had an idea and drew two more crosses on the map.

"Interesting." The priest contemplated the crosses.

"Right? Maybe the puzzle is not about the places where the bodies are found, but about where the girls live!" Agitated, Bastian sorted through his documents. "I'm pretty convinced that each of the numbers *6 7 8 9* represents one side of the city wall."

The priest nodded in agreement. "The *6* signifies the shortest segment in the south, followed by *7* in the north, *8* in the west, and *9* for the longest segment in the east."

"Elisabeth didn't live close to the southern wall—though that's what we would assume, considering that Hellenbroich carved a *1*, a *6*, and the letter *K* into her scalp."

Bastian shook his head. Something didn't fit.

"What if the letter *K* represents her last name?" the priest said quietly.

"You could be right," replied Bastian. "I haven't looked at Gertrud's body yet. I will do that first thing tomorrow!"

With these words he rose to his feet.

"If we are right, she should have an *M* carved into her scalp— and," he paused, suddenly remembering something, "the presence of the *M* in the series on the Juddeturm door makes this even more likely!"

Bastian thanked his old mentor for the help and the wine, and he said good-bye. What he didn't say was that he was thinking about the future murders that were likely to happen. The city wall consisted of four segments. Did Dietrich Hellenbroich really intend to sacrifice one girl for each segment? The ghastly thought haunted Bastian as he walked, shivering, from the church to his house.

.   .   .

The following day, Bastian went to see Doctor Josef Hesemann in his house on Grünwaldstraße. Gertrud's body lay in the vestibule of Josef's house, for the bone-chilling January blasts made it impossible to conduct the examination in the courtyard as they had done with Elisabeth.

Josef had sent his wife and their little daughter Agnes to stay with the grandparents for a week. The risk of having sweet, wild Agnes storm through the house and happen upon Gertrud's body was too high. A month ago, she would have seen Elisabeth laid out in the yard if Bastian had not had the presence of mind to quickly block the innocent girl's view.

Bastian looked pale, and, knowing how he took every crime case to heart, Josef suspected that he had been up all night brooding. Josef held Bastian in high esteem and always believed what he said. But in the past few weeks, even Josef couldn't stand Bastian's dark premonitions about Hellenbroich any longer. Like most of the townspeople, convinced that Dietrich Hellenbroich was long gone, he had simply stopped listening. Josef would never have guessed that the killer would strike another time. Unfortunately, Bastian had been right all along.

Never before had Zons seen two murders in just one month. The young, ambitious city guard had anticipated the second murder yet had been helpless to prevent it, and his torment was engraved in his face and evident in his entire demeanor. Bastian's blond hair was even more disheveled than usual, and there were dark circles under his eyes. On his unshaven face his lips were pale, almost blood-less. Yet, with his high, aristocratic-looking cheekbones and deep-set brown eyes, Bastian attracted women from every tier of their small society—Josef knew this from his cousin. But Bastian seemed blithely unaware of his attractiveness and had always remained faithful to his one love. Josef smiled to himself. As a young lad, he would certainly have been different, had God given him those smashing good looks. Instead he had had to come up with the silli-est stunts if he wanted to approach a maiden. The doctor shook his head, bemused, but then checked his reveries and readied himself for the grim task ahead.

They inspected Gertrud's body. She had been such a happy, cheerful girl with sparkling blue eyes and a full head of golden blonde curls. Now, all her beauty was snuffed out. Her dead eyes looked upward, a look of desperate panic frozen within them. Nothing was left of her long blonde locks—the killer had shaved them off completely, as he had done with his first victim. Dried blood was smeared all across her scalp.

"First I want to look for any carvings on her scalp," Bastian said. Carefully, he began to soften the crusted blood with a damp linen cloth.

A few minutes later they had cleaned the bloodied scalp, and Bastian nodded to Josef in confirmation that what they expected was evident.

The pattern repeated itself: the men found two new numbers and another letter. This time the carving read: *1 7 M*. Now Bastian was convinced that *M* stood for the first letter of Gertrud's last name, Minkenberg. The symbols on Elisabeth's head had read *1 6 K*, and *K* was the first letter of that victim's last name, Kreuzer. It just had to be right! For each segment of the wall, the killer sacrificed one girl. The letters had to refer to the girls' last names. Bastian flipped through his notebook until he found the sketch he had made of Hellenbroich's carvings in the Juddeturm's heavy wooden door. Bastian read out loud: *1 6 K 1 7 M 1 8 Z.*

"I still don't understand in what order he operates, but in case the letters really stand for the girls' last names, we have to protect all the girls in Zons whose family name begins with a *Z*." Breathless, Bastian glanced at Josef. "I'll leave you to continue here and see whether you discover something that will lead us to this disgusting monster. Remember to tell me anything you find. *Anything*," he emphasized.

With these words he threw the blood-soaked linen cloth into a wicker basket next to the door and pocketed his notebook in the depths of his heavy, sleeveless leather jerkin. Bastian left Josef's house and headed directly to the church.

"Johannes, where are you?" His excited call echoed through the small church.

"Bastian, my dear son. What brings you here at so unusual an hour?" The hoarse voice rasped from behind the altar and Father Johannes appeared. Moaning, he rubbed both hands across the back that had grown hunched over the years.

"Seems like I am getting old, my dear friend," Johannes sniffed. "I can't take more than two goblets of red wine at night. So please, do me a favor. Don't raise your voice when you speak to a shepherd of the church—and especially one who is suffering from a little overindulgence."

Painstakingly, Father Johannes sank down on one of the church benches.

"I don't think it's red wine," Bastian replied, "I think you shouldn't spend all day in the church in this infernal cold, that's my opinion. Winter is not good for your aching back. Staying near a warm fire would serve you much better."

"I know, dear Bastian, but how could I not follow the call of duty? As a diligent servant of the Lord, I must make sacrifices."

Bastian sat down next to Johannes and asked him for a list with the family names of all the young girls of Zons.

The priest got up, again with considerable effort, and with a short nod motioned Bastian to follow him. They entered a small vestibule where Johannes began searching through a big trunk. After a while he produced a huge book and leafed through it.

"This church register has a record of every birth, baptism, wedding, and death in Zons. If you go back far enough, you will find all the names you need and can copy them."

He handed the heavy book to Bastian along with a blank piece of paper and a quill pen.

"It's been a while since you last practiced writing. This will function as a long-needed exercise for you!" He patted Bastian's shoulder and waved him over to a small desk in a corner.

Bastian obliged. Numerous names and events were listed in the book, and he knew it would take him several hours to compile the list. But that didn't matter, when the time and effort could save the next girl's life—or, rather, the next two girls' lives. Even though Hellenbroich had only carved three numbers into the door of his prison cell, Bastian was convinced that he intended to kill four girls. Just like there were four segments to the city wall, there had to be four dead girls in order for Hellenbroich's murderous madness to come to fruition.

. . .

"Josef?" Bastian looked up from his writing to see the doctor, Josef Hesemann, appear in the doorframe of the church's small vestibule.

"I figured I would find you here. You told me to tell you if I found any clues, and I wanted to share an important detail I came upon while examining Gertrud's body."

Bastian stretched his sore right hand and rubbed his reddened eyes. The candles didn't provide enough light in this dark room, where the air was dry and dusty. Having spent hours here, he was almost done with his list and so absorbed in his task that he had forgotten his plea to Josef.

"Listen, Josef. I've compiled almost all the relevant names. So far, there are five girls whose last names begin with a *Z*."

"That sounds good." The doctor encouraged him with a smile before he continued, grabbing Bastian's upper arm. "Listen, Bastian. I found something odd bound within the folds of the linen gown wrapped around Gertrud, and when I saw this, I examined the gown Elisabeth was wrapped in."

Josef showed Bastian the two linen gowns. The one that had been wrapped around Gertrud had clumps of something doughlike within the creases.

Bastian frowned as he tried to make sense of this. He recalled what the old psychic had told him on Hellenbroich's farm, about Hellenbroich's obsession with the walls and towers of Zons. He held the candlelight closer to the clumped material on the cloth.

"Come here, Josef," Bastian said excitedly. "See for yourself. I'm sure these clumps are made of flour." As a miller's son, Bastian certainly knew the substance in all its permutations.

"Yes, indeed," Josef replied, and he rubbed his finger through one of the drier, caked bits of fabric to see the substance crumble into a floury pile.

"But why on earth would Hellenbroich be dragging a body through the mill?" asked Josef.

"Or maybe the tower next to the mill, the Mühlenturm," Bastian said. "The old clairvoyant expected Hellenbroich to climb up on each of the four towers."

Bastian kept thinking. Why, of course. The killer would need to visit each one of those towers. Young Gertrud happened to live next door to the Mühlenturm. He had probably killed her in the vicinity of her house, wrapped her corpse in the linen gown, and dragged her down to the river. The ground around the Mühlenturm was white from all the fine flour dust, which is why the flour had collected in the folds of the fabric as poor Gertrud's body was dragged across the ground there. Then, when she was dunked in the Rhine, the flour remnants must have formed into these doughy lumps.

"If he really picks the girls according to their last names, he must plan his crimes meticulously. Maybe in his twisted mind he thinks he needs to bring his sacrifices—the girls—as close as possible to the respective tower in order to awaken some kind of divine powers."

"But how are the numbers related to the killings?" Josef asked.

"I assume he wants to kill four girls. The first victim represents the shortest segment of the wall. She has a 6 carved into her scalp. The second victim gets a 7. The 1 could mean that he brings one sacrifice for each segment of the wall. Or, more precisely, for each of our city wall's main towers. It's from the towers that he hopes to receive the divine powers on the nights of the full moon."

"So we have three weeks to find the killer," Josef concluded.

"Right. The night of the next full moon. That's when he will prey on one of these five girls here on my list. Let's track him down before that happens, so help us God!"

. . .

69

The cold made Bastian miserable. It was early February and more bitter and raw than ever. He began to wonder why he had been crazy enough to volunteer to tiptoe along the city wall in the middle of a freezing winter night, without even a torch to warm him and light his way. But he'd taken on the task because he was convinced that Dietrich Hellenbroich had left no stone unturned when he'd planned his murders, and that he would decide to visit every single house owned by a family whose last name began with a *Z* and who had a daughter. There were five potential victims, and Bastian wanted to sense what the killer sensed when inspecting the five houses at night. Maybe this way he could anticipate Hellenbroich's next moves, while watching out for the victims at the same time.

It was way past midnight, and not a living soul was out. In this stark cold, even the soldiers from the city guard didn't patrol after midnight. They sat in the small chambers above the city gates, where, close to warm fires, it was easier to get through the night shift.

The night was utterly silent. On some days the smacking of the waves of the Rhine, rolling over the pebbled banks, was clearly audible, but this night was as noiseless as it was dark. Bastian could hardly discern his own hands in front of his face and had to concentrate not to stumble and make missteps that would echo in the eerie quiet. Each carefully tiptoed step reached his ears at such a brutal volume that he feared he'd startle all the inhabitants of Zons from their sleep. But he knew very well that one could imagine all sorts of things at night, and he calmed down. Most likely, nobody heard his steps, which was good because Bastian had resolved to climb the closest tower, the Zollturm.

Down on the street, Bastian couldn't hear or see anything in the impenetrable dark. Even the night's shadows seemed frozen. The chilly nocturnal air seeped under his jerkin, and he felt himself growing colder with every step. Cautiously, he walked up the stairs of the Zollturm, trying to glide as softly as a cat. When he had almost reached the top he saw a shadow moving, and for a moment his heart stopped beating.

What was that? He reached for the sword tucked into his belt and silently pulled the blade. He crouched on the remaining steps to the top. The platform was empty. But Bastian was sure he had seen something. He walked to the edge of the tower and glanced down.

At precisely that moment, he heard a loud cracking and felt a leather whip fly around his neck. He almost choked as the whip tightened, relentlessly pulling him to the ground. With all his force he resisted the pull and tried to sever the leather with his sword. But the sword was too long and got stuck between the bricks of the wall. He tried to loosen it but couldn't move backward. Then Bastian suddenly saw a figure detaching itself forcefully from the tower. That devil had been waiting for him, hanging on the outside wall of the tower. That's how he had surprised Bastian.

Now the other man stood behind him, pressing his own sword against Bastian's back.

"Are you following me, Bastian Mühlenberg?" a hoarse voice hissed in his ear.

"Who are you and what are you doing here?" Bastian demanded.

"I could ask you that very same question!" the voice answered, putting even more pressure on the sword pressed to Bastian's back.

Trying to focus, Bastian took a deep breath. He twisted around abruptly and knocked the sword out of his aggressor's hand.

It sailed down the first upper steps of the stairs. The two men dove to the ground in an attempt to grab it. Violently entangled, they fell down the staircase. Where the staircase made a curve, Bastian dashed against the wall at full speed. The last thing he saw was a limping person lifting a sword, prepared to strike and tumbling toward him. Then he lost consciousness.

. . .

Bastian was dreaming. He had fallen down the Zollturm and smashed hard against the floor. He waited to confront death, but death didn't come. Instead he saw a wonderful young woman. She was sitting on a bench at the Rhine and had fallen asleep despite the cold. Her face was placid and magnificently beautiful, with dark lashes on her closed eyelids and voluptuous, curving lips. A faint shimmer of melancholy lingered on her face, and he could even see tears making their way down her cheeks. The soft sadness touched Bastian's heart; he simply had to protect her even though he had never seen her before. He had never set eyes on any other woman but Marie—but this sad, sleeping girl stirred up a longing inside him that he had never felt before.

Her head was moving slowly; she seemed to be waking up. Bastian withdrew quickly into the shadows and watched her. When she opened her eyes, Bastian was startled at their color—green, and gleaming in the dark like two sparkling emeralds. How could he possibly recognize the color of her eyes, from such a distance and in this darkness, he wondered. Suddenly, a sharp pain brought him back to the ground at the foot of the Zollturm. Puzzled, Bastian looked about. Where did the emerald-eyed maiden go? His dreaming self returned, and he felt himself lifted from the ground and soaring. His body felt hot, but a comfortable draft of cool air soothed his sweating skin. With bewilderment he realized he was floating in a blue summer sky. Bastian gazed up at the welcome sun, and the blazing sunlight dissolved his consciousness.

"He is dreaming, but he's alive. He will live." Josef Hesemann comforted the sobbing young woman who was sitting at Bastian's bed holding his hand.

"Are you really sure, Josef?" she asked warily, her eyes filled with tears.

"Absolutely, Marie. I promise you, he'll be back in good shape just in time for the wedding. He was damned lucky that he didn't break his neck when he fell."

XIII.
Present

Emily was working against the clock. Well, actually, the clock had already won. She had to submit her article in one hour.

"Damn. Damn. Damn!" she hissed. Initially she'd planned to reveal the solution of the puzzle at the beginning of her article, but she still hadn't managed to actually solve it, despite all the documents from the county archive. Her idea was to launch right into the explanation of how the constellation of Corvus was linked to the layout of the city walls in Zons, and that the medieval killer had chosen his victims according to that pattern. She wanted to do something different and unusual, shifting the end up to the beginning, but so far she was struggling with it.

It seemed she did have to deliver the solution to the fatal puzzle in the end after all. Fortunately, the other two parts of her series were already finished. Each described the murder of a young woman. The first one dealt with Elisabeth Kreuzer and would be published in a few days. This part was the one the *Rheinische Post* expected in less than an hour for copyediting. She stopped ruminating about the puzzle's solution and instead went over her style and spelling one last time. She thought she had done a really good job and hoped that the article would draw a lot of interest. After reading a first draft, her editor had been impressed with her writing and promised to place the text prominently. In fact, he had assured her she'd get an entire page.

She thought, a little smugly, about how proud she'd be once all her classmates had read the article. Having a major paper devote an entire page to a first article was not a given. Most young journalists had to start far more modestly. Worst-case scenario, they had to cover local sports; thank God that was not her lot.

An hour later she hit "Send" and sighed in relief. She poured herself a glass of pinot noir and sipped it happily. Now she had the rest of the evening to spend finally solving that damned puzzle.

After a whole bottle of pinot, however, Emily was still chasing the solution. It bothered her that the decisive piece was still missing. The map of the city of Zons was spread out in front of her. Meticulous by habit, she had marked all the places where bodies had been found plus the first letters of the two victims' family names. But she still couldn't understand why these two women specifically had been attacked first.

Bastian Mühlenberg's scribblings were hard to decipher. Sometimes she could only guess the meaning of a word. She was quite good at reading old German script, but Bastian Mühlenberg surely had never won a prize for beautiful penmanship.

Irritated and exhausted, she shoved the map to the side and switched on the TV. She zapped through a few channels and got stuck with N24, a public TV channel airing a documentary about the forty-eight constellations of classical astronomy described by Ptolemy.

And suddenly, she knew the solution. Why, she should have seen this a while ago! Again she skimmed Bastian's notes, now comprehending more of his chicken scratch. She started up her computer and downloaded a map of the constellations in the northern sky. Then she printed out the constellations of the Raven and Virgo. She laid the map of the constellations on top of the city map, which she turned clockwise. But still she didn't see what she had hoped to see. Then a new idea crossed her mind.

She stood up and walked over to her bookcase, which had a giant old reference book on astronomy, one she'd kept since childhood. Next she went to a drawer of sketchbooks and art supplies to fetch some tracing paper. The book's index quickly led her to a map of Ptolemy's constellations. She laid the book flat and pressed the paper against it, tracing a map of the stars. Again she laid the transparent map over the city map, which she turned clockwise once more—and then she saw it.

The numbers *6 7 8 9* represented the order in which the victims were killed. But the letters still wouldn't fit. Argh! She'd have to plow through the last pages of Bastian's notes after all. She had hoped to avoid it, but it seemed she had no choice. Still, at least she'd begun to understand the chronological order of the murders. She had solved a part of the puzzle!

Emily's triumph gave her a second wind. Concentrating deeply, she looked at the dot on the city map that marked the house of the third victim. Something about it seemed familiar. But between that bottle of wine, the stress over the copyediting deadline, and the late hour, she couldn't seem to force to the surface the idea that was percolating in her mind. Only when she was already in bed and dreaming peacefully did the revelation shoot into Emily's consciousness. Abruptly she sat up and opened her eyes.

"It's Anna's house!"

· · ·

Oliver Bergmann's sleep was rudely interrupted by the loud ringing of his cell. He blinked. What time was it? Only half past six. Who dared to call so early in the morning? He could have slept at least another half hour. It was probably his mom, who was simply too excited about the imminent weekend. What could she want now? Oliver sighed. He got up and walked to his phone.

It wasn't his mother but Klaus, speaking quickly and urgently. "Oliver, come to the precinct as fast as you can. The boss just called me. He told me to get you here on the double. We have a body in Zons, a woman, and we're putting together a special commission as we speak."

Fifteen minutes later, Oliver and Klaus sat in their boss's office. Hans Steuermark looked concerned.

"According to the local officers, the woman was badly mangled," he told the two detectives. "From what we can tell so far, she was tortured and possibly raped as well. She hasn't been identified yet. A jogger found her early this morning. The killer—or maybe the killers—tied her to a chain and suspended her on one of those old towers at the Schlossplatz. I'm assigning you both to the case, and I want you to get cracking this instant!" He dismissed them.

Usually the drive between Neuss and Zons took about ten to fifteen minutes, depending on whether one took the Autobahn or the country road. Klaus opted for the supposedly faster Autobahn A57.

"I really hope we'll have more luck with this body than with the Body in the Woods," Klaus said and hit the gas pedal.

"Yep, a bit more luck would look good for us," Oliver agreed and looked out the window.

His adrenaline had been pumping since Klaus had called him; he couldn't wait to arrive at the crime scene. But as was so often the case, the A57 was under construction, and they advanced slowly. It took them almost thirty minutes to reach Zons.

They parked directly on the Schlossplatz, near the well-preserved city wall, and jumped out of the car.

"I haven't been back here since I was a boy," Klaus said and looked up to the edge of the wall.

"Same here. It's been many years. I've always liked this medieval city," Oliver answered.

"It wouldn't be easy to scale those walls," Klaus mused. "You'd need a ladder, or at least a rope with iron hooks on it."

Through a small gate they walked to the other side of the city wall. The green Rhine meadows spread out directly in front of them, several majestic old willow trees lining the path. On this cold, barren December day, the sight was a blessing to the eye. Neuss didn't have that much nature to offer, especially not all in one place like this.

About a dozen young children were skating on a natural ice rink amid the peaceful landscape, some eighty yards from where Klaus and Oliver stood. The shallow basin was probably a relic from the last flood. A small boy lost his balance and toppled onto the ice. He looked up, his face deep red, and screamed for his mother, who now hurried over to comfort her tearful little skater. Oliver smiled as he watched the scene. He used to love ice-skating when he was a boy, and of course his helicopter mom had followed him everywhere, making sure that nothing happened to her precious son.

Klaus tapped him on the shoulder and roused him from his musings. Oliver turned around and saw the corpse hanging from the tower, the Krötschenturm. He looked back at the playing children.

"Klaus, this area needs to be widely sealed off. Those kids haven't noticed yet, but any moment now we'll have cops and the forensics team and blue and red lights all over the place. I don't want *any* of those kids to see that dangling corpse."

"Good call, Oliver. Let me radio this right now. We should probably seal off the area around this entire segment of the wall. People like to go for walks here; we'll be dealing with hundreds of gawkers if we don't clear the area." Klaus reached for his radio.

Oliver approached the corpse and stiffened for a moment. The chain was attached to one arm, and the body was swaying slightly in the wind. A superficial glance might have suggested it was only an oversized flour sack hanging from the tower, because the dead woman was entirely wrapped in a rough, cream-colored linen gown. Oliver couldn't see a face because the body was hanging with its back toward him. He was just wondering how the jogger could have known the victim's gender, when a heavy gust of wind made the chain twist around, creaking loudly. The corpse swayed slowly back and forth, pivoting around its own axis with each new gust of wind, until it had turned 180 degrees and its red, empty eyes stared directly at Oliver.

Oh, dear God! The victim's lower jaw was hanging down lopsided, clearly broken. Her tongue was bluish-black and stuck halfway out of her lopsided mouth. As far as Oliver could tell with all the blood in her mouth, she was missing several teeth. Dried blood was smeared across her battered face. It looked as if someone had poured red paint down from the top of her head, where it had dried and caked in runnels.

"I've never seen anything so horrible," Klaus murmured from behind.

"Yeah," Oliver answered. "Compared to this, our Body in the Woods was a natural death."

That earlier victim had displayed no visible signs of torture; he had obviously been killed within seconds and probably hadn't suffered. This poor woman, however, looked as if she had endured excruciating torment before she died.

79

Within the area, now sealed off from onlookers, the team from Forensics was already busy, illuminating the corpse with a whirlwind of flashlights as if the dead woman was a model in a fashion show. Other members from the unit, dressed completely in white with latex gloves on, searched the ground beneath her feet using small forceps. They stored each piece of evidence in a small plastic bag, carefully labeling them, and stacked the bags in a large box to bring back to the lab.

Almost thirty minutes passed before they were done and the corpse could finally be taken off the hook. Anxiously, Oliver and Klaus stood aside until the woman had been placed on a gurney and they could approach her. Beneath the old-fashioned gown, she was fully dressed. She even wore jeans.

Maybe we were wrong and it wasn't rape, Oliver thought.

There was dirt under her ragged, broken fingernails, but her head looked far worse. Her hair had been shaved off. From the remains of her eyebrows, they assumed she had been brunette. Her scalp was smeared with blood and scattered with dark-rimmed wounds. Apparently, the killer had cut deeply into her scalp in several places.

What a gruesome way to torture someone, Oliver thought.

As if reading his mind, Klaus chimed in, "Can you even imagine? Sitting there defenseless and chained while a lunatic carves up your scalp and you feel your own blood running over your face?"

Oliver turned away in horror—it was too ghastly to consider.

"We'll take her to Forensics and perform the autopsy today," one of the medical examiners informed them. He swiftly zipped the body bag and prepared the woman's body for transport.

.   .   .

An hour later, back at the precinct, Oliver and Klaus reported to their boss.

"Any clues that could help us identify the woman?" Steuermark asked.

They shook their heads slightly. No.

"The woman was fully dressed, but we couldn't find any ID or purse on her," Klaus said.

"Fully dressed. So probably not a rape?"

"Yes, fully dressed," Klaus affirmed. "Only her shoes are missing. They could have slipped off her feet during the transport. Maybe she never wore any. We asked Forensics to look out for shoes. If they fell off while he was transporting her, we might find a trace that'll lead us directly to the place where the killer tortured and murdered her."

Oliver added, "The coroner examined the skin on her wrist where the chain was attached; his initial finding is that she was already dead when the murderer suspended her at the tower. He said her limbs were barely swollen, which indicates her heart had already stopped beating by the time he tied her to the chain."

"Seems our killer wanted us to find her as soon as possible," Steuermark said. "Otherwise he wouldn't have exposed her at such a public location. Of course, we're assuming that the killer is male, based on prior cases and the strength it would've taken to carry out this monstrous deed."

He recalled the case of a serial killer from many years ago. That guy, too, had wanted his acts to be widely seen. The gruesome exhibitions of his victims regularly shocked the public, gripping the entire county with a paralyzing, spreading fear of his atrocities. It was common for serial killers to present their victims as conspicuously as possible, and often they would mingle with the crowd of onlookers, enthralled by their "work of art" and their own power.

Steuermark wished he was wrong in suspecting that this murder would not be the last such one. He really had no use for another serial killer now, especially in light of the most recent crime statistics that had been published last week and that had forced him to appear in a hastily called press conference to explain the stark rise of violent crimes in the region. In fact, it wasn't a surprise at all that crime had gone up in the past two years, since the state government had cut the budget dramatically, forcing him to reduce his manpower. It was only thanks to his excellent relations with the North Rhine–Westphalian Office of Criminal Investigations that Steuermark had been able to add Oliver Bergmann to his team of detectives.

.   .   .

Emily was crestfallen. As she leafed through the latest issue of the *Rheinische Post*, she had to force herself to not scream out loud. She had expected to be published on one of the main pages of the Style or Culture sections—but instead, that ass of an editor had exiled her great article to one of the last pages of the issue.

And not only that, they'd given it so little space that all the reader saw was a headline and a reference to a feature series "coming soon." Why had she pulled one all-nighter after another? Why had she forced herself to finish the first part of her article on time while battling the flu, and why had the newspaper pressured her so much when all they printed in the end were these pathetic few lines?

She could hardly believe it—and all because of a recent murder in Zons. Some woman found dead and unidentified. Frustrated, Emily slam-dunked the paper into the trash. There was news about homicides in Germany every day. Most of the murders committed weren't even covered at all—otherwise there'd be no space left for other stories. And now this one murder in a tiny town like Zons had postponed her first publication!

. . .

The investigations were running at warp speed—but still not fast enough. Since the discovery of the dead woman a week ago, more than five hundred witness statements had been filed, and Oliver and Klaus were under the gun. Steuermark had to appear almost daily in multiple press conferences about the ongoing investigations, and now the mayor from Dormagen was also on their case.

Zons was incorporated in the nearby city of Dormagen, an idyllic medieval tourist attraction. The mayor was worried about the long-term reputation of his city, fearing a sudden drop in tourism. He was convinced that if he were running the show, the murder would have been solved in one day. He had little sympathy for the slow progress they were making.

The Body in the Woods case had been pushed into the background, and Oliver couldn't say he was particularly sad about it. The atmosphere in the precinct, however, was extremely tense. One could almost see the detectives duck their heads when Hans Steuermark paced through the office, as he was now doing at regular intervals, always asking for the latest status report.

While Steuermark was known as the good-hearted chief of the Crime Commission who always had a friendly ear for his employees' troubles, he was not known for his patience. In times like these, when he asked for results that could not be delivered, you needed a thick skin to deal with him.

Klaus had faced this truth yesterday, when the woman's identity had been confirmed. He had been out to lunch with his girlfriend and hadn't learned about the identification until an hour later. Unfortunately, that was half an hour after Hans Steuermark had heard the news. The entire office witnessed the eruption that followed Klaus's return. Poor Klaus. The roasting obliterated his post-lunch good mood and turned his normally erect bearing into a subdued and shrunken cringe.

The dead woman was one Michelle Peters, single, twenty-five years old. She had moved to Zons about a year ago, after having inherited her grandmother's small, old house with rustic charm on Mauerstraße, next to the city wall and the Krötschenturm. Apparently the grandmother had left Michelle a considerable amount of cash assets, since the little house had recently been renovated.

Michelle Peters was from southern Germany. She had only been living in Zons for a short period, and nobody noticed her absence at first. When her family and employer were unable to reach her for a week, they filed a missing-persons report. The detectives got lucky when Peters's father came to town; the description of the hair color, height, and weight of the murder victim matched his daughter's, and he insisted on coming in to view the body. What he saw broke him utterly but moved the investigation along for Oliver and Klaus.

By now they had also determined what had caused her death. The killer had strangled her with his own hands. Forensics had even been able to identify the brand of latex gloves he had used—though unfortunately it was a very common brand, available in a retail chain that was prominent throughout the South. So far, it seemed that the killer had acted with a great deal of precaution and not left behind any DNA.

But the forensic examinations were not yet complete. The origin of some filaments found on the linen gown still needed to be determined, and Oliver, assuming that the killer had not carried the victim on his back, hoped those fibers might reveal something about the vehicle in which Michelle Peters had been transported to the tower in Zons. Even though she lived only a stone's throw from the tower, it seemed clear from an inspection of her apartment—which showed no evidence of a struggle—that Peters had been taken elsewhere, killed, and brought back to the tower.

Another important finding was that it was not a sexual assault. The victim's hair had been shaved, and she had been brutally battered, but there was no sign of sexual activity. And the killer had not carved into the scalp at random, with the goal of simply causing pain. Very deliberately, he had carved letters and numbers into the woman's scalp, three of them: *1 6 K*. The significance of these symbols eluded the police entirely. Needless to say, this finding was kept extremely confidential. The media had only been fed unimportant facts.

XIV.
Five Hundred Years Ago

Bastian's head was throbbing. He wanted to open his eyes, but his lids were as heavy as millstones, and he felt oppressively hot. His whole body was bathed in sweat. He could feel someone placing a cool, damp cloth on his head, and he heard a male voice.

"Bastian, can you hear me? Bastian . . . Bastian?" The speaker sounded concerned, and Bastian tried to think of whose voice it was. Very slowly, he managed to open his eyes a sliver.

"Where am I?" he asked hoarsely.

"In my house," Josef Hesemann answered in a calm and caring tone. "You were so ill I wanted to have you under my vigilant care around the clock. You are suffering from a serious head injury, and you've been unconscious so long we worried you might not recover."

"How long was I unconscious?" Bastian asked. Suddenly, he could open his eyes all the way and saw Josef smiling at him.

"More than two weeks, my friend. Your sweet Marie was getting all worried about the wedding, but I promised her to have you fixed before that!"

Bastian tried to sit up in his bed, but he fell back against the pillows. Still, he managed to squeeze Josef's hand and said, "Josef, I saw him!"

"Who did you see, Bastian?"

"Dietrich Hellenbroich!"

"He was the one who threw you down the stairs of the Zollturm?"

"Yes, I surprised him there. We fought. I almost had him, but then I lost my balance and must have fallen. I thought he'd kill me."

Josef frowned.

"Indeed, it is strange that he didn't, Bastian."

"The last thing I remember is how he was approaching me with my own sword in his hand. I was lying helplessly on the lower steps and couldn't move. I was sure he'd beat me to death."

Then he suddenly looked about him, agitated.

"Where is my jerkin?" He was shocked when he realized he was naked under the heavy cover.

"Calm down, dear Bastian." Softly, Josef pushed him back onto the bed. "You need to take it easy and rest. You're still badly injured. If you get up too fast, you'll get dizzy and possibly fall into a faint again—who knows for how long."

"Please, Josef, search through my jerkin. In one of the pockets you should find a list of those five girls whose last names start with a *Z*. We need to bring them to a safe place before the killer strikes again. I don't believe we'll catch him before the next full moon."

Josef searched Bastian's clothes, eventually finding the heavy sleeveless vest and drawing a thin, crumpled sheet of paper from one of the inner pockets.

"This one?" he asked, slowly unfolding it.

"Yes, it contains the five names. Tell me, Josef, when is the next full moon?"

Josef thought for a moment. "In five days, I believe. That leaves us enough time."

"Yes," Bastian agreed. "This time, he won't kill another girl. Please let the girls know that they have to spend the upcoming full moon night in Father Johannes's custody. We will have the soldiers from the City Guard encircle the church and lock the gates so that nobody can get in or out of the city. Even if Dietrich Hellenbroich tries to break into the walls, we'll be there to greet him. And if we don't catch him, at least we'll have prevented him from killing a third victim. Then he might leave Zons in peace!"

Exhausted, Bastian leaned back deeply into his pillows, overwhelmed by the powerful urge to sleep.

.   .   .

It was another raw, frigid night in the seemingly endless winter. Gradually the moon was growing into a big, yellow circle. Dietrich stood at the window and looked toward Zons. Soon, his time would come again. The sheer thought stirred his blood in anticipation. This time it would be especially exciting. There was a reason he had changed his mind at the last minute and let that meddlesome city guard survive. He could have rammed the man's own sword deep into his heart, but what purpose could a dead Bastian Mühlenberg serve him? With a worthy challenger, the puzzle was even more gratifying to create.

Since that night when he'd sneaked into the church and spied on Bastian and the priest discussing his grandiose "fatal puzzle," he had felt irrepressible pride. Granted, the two were not too far off in their reasoning—but they had overlooked a decisive piece of the puzzle, even though it was in plain sight right before their eyes. *Hah!* Bastian thought he could prevent Dietrich from finishing his so-called fatal puzzle, but Dietrich grinned to think just how wrong the miller's son was.

Deep in thought, he rubbed his amulet. He would have to pay the smuggler soon. The amulet had belonged to his father, and even though he hated the man from the bottom of his heart, he was attached to this family heirloom. Yet the only way to get in and out of Zons was to curry favor with the smugglers. It had taken him some effort to locate the most successful smuggler gang, but in a dark tavern close to the river he'd finally found them. After he'd treated them to several barrels of mead, they'd struck a deal.

A faint feeling of regret swept through Dietrich as he remembered little Gertrud. Her hair so beautiful, long and blonde; her skin so soft and innocent. He recalled the hope that had been shining in her eyes until the very last moment. But God had not come to her rescue. As always, God had abandoned his little lamb. In turn He had helped Dietrich to satisfy his lust and feel like a true warrior. He regretted only that this beauty had not been exposed at the tower for all to see, as his first conquest had been. A pack of wolves had attacked them when he was dragging the girl deeper into the Rhine meadows, forcing him to change his plan. He would have loved to pay her his last respects, but the wolves had almost overwhelmed him. Dietrich got lucky when he managed to stab one of the wolves in its flank. The wolf howled loudly, and his spilt blood attracted the other wolves' attention, and they abandoned Dietrich. Howling, the animals disappeared into the darkness of the woods from which they had come and where, Dietrich assumed, they'd feast on the injured one.

. . .

Three days later, Bastian was still confined to bed. While he managed to sit upright for a few hours, there was no way he could stand on his feet. Nevertheless, all the preparations for the coming full moon were completed. Each of the five girls had been brought to

Josef's house where Bastian himself had spoken with them, explaining the gravity of the matter. They had all stared at him with wide and fearful eyes and promised they'd spend the entire night together inside the church. At no time was any of them to be alone. They would even have to go relieve themselves in pairs.

Bastian had also personally briefed the soldiers from the City Guard. He still resented their sloppy performance four weeks ago, when they had disobeyed his orders. Had his men been more responsible, Gertrud Minkenberg might still be alive. If any one of them went about his guard duties without the appropriate care, dedication, and commitment, Bastian would fire him from the squadron and expel him from Zons. His men looked at him remorsefully, and Bastian was convinced that this time they'd all give their lives if necessary in order to catch Dietrich Hellenbroich.

Yes, everything was prepared. The killer would come and fall right into their trap.

XV.
Present

Emily and Anna were enjoying some spare time in a café called Altes Zollhaus. They had ordered two large lattes and were leafing through the *Rheinische Post*. A triumphant smile curled around Emily's lips. This morning, at long last, the first part of her series had been published: "Fatal Puzzle: The Historic Murder Cases of Zons. Part I by Emily Richter." A large, flattering photo even accompanied her byline.

They had made her wait three weeks, but in the end it had been well worth the wait. The excitement about the recent murder in Zons had died down, and by now any news of the case was run on the last pages of the Local section.

Emily's story, however, was prominently featured on the cover of the Culture section. Beaming with pride, Emily observed two women at a neighboring table who were discussing the killer and his puzzle. Both were in Zons for the first time and intended to visit the places described in the article.

"Have you solved the puzzle yet?" Anna's question interrupted Emily's thoughts.

Emily shook her head. No, she had not been able to decipher the last pages of Bastian's notebook. At some point it must have gotten wet—the ink was smudged, which made his old German handwriting, already hard to read, basically illegible. Emily had searched the Internet and found a company that specialized in the restoration of historic texts. They would eliminate the smudgy ink spots and make blowups of the respective pages. They promised her that after the treatment, 80 percent of the text would be legible. Emily was expecting the prints any day now.

She was extremely anxious, because presumably those prints would finally help her understand the killer's actions, and her research into the medieval murders would put to rest a long-held myth. Her article would be a respected piece of evidence proving that sick serial killers were not exclusively a phenomenon of modern society, but a problem that had existed many centuries ago on every continent. Granted, a single article would not be enough by scientific standards, but Emily was already dreaming about her future research on serial killers all over Europe and across the centuries. One step at a time, she told herself. First she'd have to solve this puzzle, the puzzle created by a killer in Zons five hundred years ago.

.   .   .

Fascinated, Oliver Bergmann stared at the front page of the Culture section in the *Rheinische Post*. A beautiful young woman with a mysterious smile stared back at him. Usually he wasn't particularly interested in the Culture section, but today it opened with an article about a string of murders in medieval Zons. At first he'd only read the article hoping to find out more about the journalist, the intriguing-looking woman in the picture, but the more he read, the more familiar the story sounded. Oliver frowned.

Quietly, Klaus stepped up behind him.

"She's cute. Are you reading or ogling?" Teasing, he poked Oliver in the side. Oliver blushed slightly and put the newspaper on the table.

"You should read this, Klaus. Somehow the description of the body reminds me of Michelle Peters."

Klaus burst into laughter and shook his head. "Right, Oliver. Not only are we suddenly dealing with a copycat killer who's re creating a medieval crime, but also our top priority is to interrogate the pretty writer on page one of today's Culture section!"

Oliver looked at Klaus. "You know what? That's exactly what we should do today."

"What is it you two should do today?"

Startled, they turned around and saw a testy Hans Steuermark glaring at them. Oliver checked his watch. Not even ten o'clock. Too early for Steuermark's ritualistic patrol. The guys from Interior were probably breathing down his neck because the investigations in the Michelle Peters case were stalling.

Steuermark grabbed the paper from Oliver's desk and began reading the article.

"Unbelievable," he muttered after a few minutes and pressed the paper into Klaus's hand. "You better listen to what your partner says. Read this!"

Confused, Klaus looked from Oliver to Steuermark before he followed his boss's orders and skimmed the article.

The dead woman from the past had indeed not only suffered the same injuries as Michelle Peters, but also had the same numbers and letter carved into her scalp. *1 6 K.* How was that possible?

"We need to find out where this information is published and who had access to it. Start with Emily Richter!" Hans Steuermark turned abruptly and stomped out of the office.

.   .   .

Anna was on the verge of tears. Only a little while ago she had been enjoying life, chatting with Emily over lattes and Emily's article, and now all her cheer had disappeared. She should never have opened the mailbox. She'd known it was coming, had tried to brace herself for this moment. Now that it had actually happened, she was overwhelmed with grief. How many times had she pictured herself with the damned postcard between thumb and index finger, walking directly to the trashcan, and drawing a final line through her relationship with Martin?

The postcards had been their little game. From every vacation they spent together, they would send each other a postcard with loving words as a reminder of the days they had enjoyed. What made it even more special was that they arranged for the postcards to arrive not right away, but only after six months. They had found an online service that offered to mail their greetings with the desired delay.

The postcard she held now had been mailed from their romantic travels through Portugal. Was it only six months ago that they had been sunbathing on the beaches, surrounded by the marvelous cliffs of the Algarve coast? They both loved the sunny, southern European countries. Back then, Anna could never have imagined that Martin wouldn't be a part of her life anymore. She'd been convinced that he was the one. But oh boy, had she been wrong. Nor would she ever have dreamed that he was gay. Their sex life had been amazing—and it never seemed like Martin felt something was missing. But apparently he did. For the past five years, the man Anna thought she knew inside out had been perfectly hiding a completely different identity from her.

A wave of love swept over her as she read his fond words on the postcard. How could this all have been a lie? How had he been capable of pretending so convincingly? And why had he stayed with her for so long to begin with, when, in fact, he preferred guys? She simply could not wrap her head around it, nor would she ever.

Over the past few weeks she had actually believed she was over him. Gradually it had been easier to push aside the many questions that were haunting her. There had been entire days when she didn't think of Martin at all. Now this postcard had dragged her back into her old world of pain, and tears streamed down her cheeks.

Why did he have to cut her out of his life so completely? At first she'd been glad for the distance; it helped her keep him out of her head. But three months of absolutely no contact seemed unreasonably drastic. She would have expected him to at least be polite enough to ask her how she was doing. It seemed, though, that his new universe with Christopher in Berlin was so exciting that he had forgotten about her for good. She wondered whether he was holding her postcard in his hands at this very moment. Would he reminisce about their time together? Would he at least feel a tinge of regret?

Impulsively she grabbed her cell phone and dialed his number. It went directly to voice mail. Perhaps he was in a dead spot or his battery had died, as usual. Anna hung up, disappointed and relieved at the same time.

.   .   .

Oliver Bergmann rubbed his sweaty hands nervously against his jeans. He was in Lindenthal, a neighborhood in central Cologne, standing in front of an impressive-looking apartment building— the graduate student dorm. It was close to the university campus and as busy as the Berlin train station. The chilly temperatures hadn't kept the laughing young crowd of students inside, and the main entrance door opened and closed frequently. Oliver tried to focus and find Emily Richter's name on one of the many nameplates, but every time the door swung open, he had to step aside and lost his orientation. Finally, after studying the tiny plates with the fading handwriting for the fourth time, he found her. He took a deep breath and resolutely pushed the ringer.

A female voice crackled through the intercom. "Hello, who is it?"

"Oliver Bergmann, Crime Commission Neuss. We spoke on the phone."

"Right, please come up."

Emily Richter lived on the sixth floor of a walk-up. Once at her door, Oliver tried to wipe the sweat off his forehead and look calm. He smiled politely and followed Emily into her small studio.

Several piles of paper were stacked on a desk in one corner; the rest of the studio seemed well kept and tidy. Emily noticed Oliver glancing at her desk and apologized for the chaos.

"You know, I'm planning on writing three parts altogether about the historic murder cases. One part for each murder. But I still haven't been able to solve the puzzle that made the killer so famous back then. I leave all my research material spread out in case I need to look up something."

"No worries," Oliver reassured her. "Our desks in the precinct look the same when we're working on a case. Obviously we also have huge bulletin boards . . . but everything that somehow belongs together gets thrown in one big pile."

"May I offer you something to drink?" said Emily, in hostess mode. "Tea, maybe?"

"I'd love some, but only if it's not too much work."

Emily disappeared in the kitchen and resurfaced after a brief moment carrying a tray. Apparently she had already had the tea ready for Oliver's arrival. He was more pleased than he let on about the foresight her hospitality suggested.

"How can I be of assistance, Herr Bergmann?" Emily asked while she carefully poured him a cup of aromatic Earl Grey.

"I need to know a thing or two about your article. I've noticed a few details that could be related to the recent murder in Zons."

He bit his tongue. The crush he had developed on this beautiful and capable young woman must not make him lose his professionalism; he mustn't share with her the so-far-undisclosed facts about the murder of Michelle Peters. To date they had released only the victim's name and the cause of death. Only a few investigators in the loop knew about the shaved hair and the grisly, inscrutable carvings on her scalp.

He explained quickly the reason for his visit. Five hundred years separated the two cases, yet both victims had been found hanging from the tower at the Schlossplatz in Zons.

Oliver asked Emily where, exactly, she had done her research. She showed him all of her material and mentioned the visit to the county archive. Oliver made a note to stop by there next. It seemed highly possible that Michelle's killer had gathered his knowledge at the very same place. According to Emily, this was the only place that held descriptions and sketches of the historic corpse. One glance into the age-old notebook of that Mühlenberg guy had been sufficient to determine that the symbols on Michelle Peters's scalp were identical to the ones on Elisabeth Kreuzer's. *1 6 K.*

His gut feeling this morning upon reading Emily Richter's article in the *Rheinische Post* had not failed him. All the details pointed to a copycat killer.

He stood, thanked Emily, and shook her hand.

"I'll send two colleagues over later to make copies of your research material."

Emily nodded attentively, and as she saw him to the door, she looked at him and smiled, her brown eyes shining. His heart flipped over. He had sensed it the moment he first looked at her photo in the newspaper. He had fallen head over heels for Emily Richter.

. . .

Back at his desk at the precinct, Oliver saw that the lab report on the filaments found on Michelle Peters's body had finally been delivered. Eagerly, he opened the envelope and began to read. No surprises but one: the filaments from the linen gown wrapped around the dead body seemed to match those of a seat cushion typically found in a Ford Mondeo, more specifically a Ford Mondeo manufactured between the years 2000 and 2003.

Alarm bells began to clang in the back of Oliver's head. Almost as if controlled by external powers, his hand reached for the Body in the Woods file on the sideboard. Witnesses had described the getaway car as a Ford Mondeo, and the respective lab report listed the same filaments. Or at least the filaments were associated with the same Mondeo production series.

Again, as if on autopilot, he dialed the number of the lab and asked the technicians to run a test to determine whether the filaments from both cases were identical. Could there really be a link between that body in the forest and the dead woman in Zons?

XVI.
Five Hundred Years Ago

It was almost midnight. Bastian felt a slight dizziness and forced himself to stand as still as possible. Wernhart stood next to him, almost as tense as Bastian. It was yet another in the long series of excruciatingly icy nights, and a full moon was shining up in the clear sky. Tonight was the night Dietrich Hellenbroich planned to kill his next victim—but this time the people of Zons were prepared.

The girls were safely locked inside the church, with each entrance—and all the city gates—secured by two men from the City Guard. An additional soldier stood watch on each tower, and Bastian had ordered that all visitors be registered at the city gates beginning even a day before the full moon. Everyone arriving or leaving had to report with his or her full name.

Bastian had further hired four scriveners—one for each gate and tower—to register the names neatly with quill and ink on thick paper scrolls. From his perspective, there was absolutely no gap for Hellenbroich to slip through into the city. In his head, Bastian went through the long list of safety measures again. No. He was sure he had considered all eventualities.

He looked up into the breathtaking night sky. The full moon was round and blinding white, and thousands of stars twinkled down. He would have loved to share this beauty in sweet togetherness with Marie. They had not seen as much of each other recently as they had in previous months. Ever since the first murder, Bastian was always busy, and even when he did spend time with Marie, his mind was preoccupied with Hellenbroich. He recalled the terrified, worried look in Marie's eyes after he'd fallen from the Zollturm. That glance held all the love she had for him, and once this nightmare was over he promised himself to spend more time with her again. She really did not deserve to be so neglected.

Wernhart interrupted his thoughts with a whispered complaint. "Damn it, my leg's asleep." Grimacing, he rubbed his right calf and tried to move his foot up and down. "What time do you think it is?" he asked Bastian.

"Should be shortly after midnight." Bastian, too, stretched his stiffening limbs.

They had spent the past six hours standing almost motionless in a small alley in front of the church, and the long, uncomfortable night was nowhere near over. Bastian himself had ordered that the guards remain on their posts until daybreak. This time they had to be on top of everything!

XVII.

Present

An entire week had passed since Anna had first tried to reach Martin on his phone, and still she had not dared tell Emily. Emily would certainly be disappointed. She thought of Anna as strong and steady, and while Anna usually fit comfortably in that role, she also knew there was a well of insecurity within her that she kept thoroughly hidden from everyone, even her best friend.

She had tried Martin's phone on a daily basis, and while she was terribly embarrassed about this, she was also growing increasingly worried. It was so not like Martin, who could not spend a second without his phone. Now it had been switched off for over a week? At first she'd figured he was in a place with no reception, but when all seven of her calls went straight to voice mail, she discarded the idea. That was too much of a coincidence.

She looked at the clock. It was a few minutes past eight in the morning. A quick glance at her BlackBerry informed her that her first business meeting was after ten. That left enough time to swing by Martin's old apartment.

Fifteen minutes later, Anna parked her car near the City Park in Neuss and walked over to one of the big old apartment buildings. The City Park was one of the most popular residential areas in Neuss. When she visited Martin, Anna had always enjoyed the lush, green surroundings.

She looked up to his windows. They were all dark. She walked to the front door and was just about to ring the bell when the door squeaked open and Martin's landlord, Herr Hengsteberg, stood in front of her, looking tired with dark circles under his eyes.

"Good morning, Herr Hengsteberg!" Anna greeted him, surprised.

"Good morning, Frau Winterfeld, how are you? I haven't seen you around in ages!"

"I've been really busy lately," Anna said evasively.

"Well, to tell you the truth, I'm glad I've run into you," Herr Hengsteberg told her. He pushed his frameless spectacles up his nose. "I haven't seen your boyfriend for months, and honestly, I'm quite annoyed with him because he still owes me last month's rent. I've just gone up to his apartment to talk with him, but he won't open the door. Let me tell you, I don't even think he's home. I've been trying for weeks, but his neighbor hasn't seen him around at all either."

"Well, to be frank, he broke up with me. I haven't had contact with him for a while. And his cell phone seems to be switched off."

"Oh, I am so sorry to hear this, Frau Winterfeld. You two were such a lovely couple. What happened?"

Anna looked down and said nothing.

"I apologize, Frau Winterfeld, I didn't mean to make you feel uncomfortable. However, I do want to know the whereabouts of your ex! You will understand that I do need the payment of the rent."

"I understand very well," Anna said quietly, and she added, "I still have a key. Why don't we take a look?"

"I was going to suggest that myself, Frau Winterfeld. I think having you here while we look is a godsend; perhaps you can find some clues to his whereabouts."

They walked up to Martin's third-floor apartment in silence. Anna had a strange feeling in her stomach. Of course, Martin had moved to Berlin with Christopher. But why had he not given Herr Hengsteberg notice? Besides, he would never be late with the rent. He was far too responsible.

Up on the third floor, the landlord separated Martin's key from all the others on his large ring. One twist of the key and the door sprang open.

Stale, stuffy air greeted them, and the faint smell of decay gave Anna a wave of nausea. She turned around and stepped back out into the hall.

Herr Hengsteberg didn't seem to mind the rotting smell. Undeterred, he walked into the apartment. Anna could hear him open the windows.

"Just wait a few minutes and the bad smell will be gone. It's probably the trash that hasn't been emptied."

Anna waited until she felt a fresh, cool breeze on her cheeks before she followed Herr Hengsteberg into Martin's apartment. Everything looked as if Martin could show up at any moment. Then she saw his wallet on the dresser in the hall and his cell phone on the kitchen table. Now she understood why she hadn't been able to reach him. The phone was off, and the battery had probably been dead for a while. The landlord was emptying the reeking trash into a large garbage bag.

"That's been taken care of," he declared, satisfied, and closed the bag with a knot.

Pale-faced, Anna sat down on a kitchen chair. The uneasy sense of foreboding she had felt all through the past week seemed to be shaping into a sad reality.

"Something's wrong, Herr Hengsteberg. Martin would never leave without his wallet and his phone."

.   .   .

With deadpan expressions on their faces, Oliver and Klaus were contemplating the neglected state of the county archive's interior. The archivist limped over to a shelf on the left side of the lobby, where he began rummaging through a box of file cards.

"Here it is!" the two detectives heard him say, his voice full of self-importance. When the two had first arrived and flashed their badges, he had suddenly felt like a celebrity. Recently, more and more people were coming to him wanting to learn about the historic murder cases and the fatal puzzle.

He limped back to the detectives and handed them the five file cards that identified each person who had borrowed the related documents.

"Nobody cared about those documents for the past ten years. But during the last nine months I have issued them to five different people!"

"We appreciate your help. This is a very important clue for us."

Oliver noted the names and the dates on which they'd borrowed the documents. Only one name on the list was familiar: Emily Richter. A brief smile flashed over his face at the thought of her.

"I'd be happy to tell you everything you want to know about the killer and his puzzle," the archivist said with a grin, puffing out his chest with pride.

"Thank you, but the list of names is enough for now."

"But you need to study the documents! Otherwise you won't be able to determine whether you really are dealing with a copycat or not!"

Perplexed, they stared at the archivist. How could he know that that's what they were trying to determine? He had certainly not read it in the papers!

"What makes you say that?"

The old archivist responded with a sullen expression and started to limp away.

"Hey, wait a moment!" Oliver yelled after him.

The old man turned around again and peered at Oliver through his enormous lenses.

"Well, over the past five hundred years, how many dead bodies do you think have been found dangling from the tower at the Schlossplatz?" He spat as he talked, droplets of spittle landing squarely on Oliver's chin. Fortunately, Klaus stepped up next to him and took over the conversation.

"Listen, Mister. We are investigating a murder case, and you are legally obligated to cooperate. So I ask you again, what makes you say it could be a copycat killer?"

The archivist sighed.

"I've just said it. Since 1495, there have only been two dead women hanging from that tower. I know the history of Zons from A to Z. Don't you think it's likely that our contemporary killer was inspired by his historic brother in spirit?"

He grabbed the *Rheinische Post* and opened it to Emily Richter's article.

"Here, see for yourself. This young lady is my most recent visitor, and she describes the murder of Elisabeth Kreuzer in great detail. I'll bet you that the same code was also carved into Michelle Peters's scalp!"

He looked at them triumphantly and waved the newspaper in front of their faces. Klaus took it from him.

"Thank you, but we are already very familiar with that article. Please continue to be at our disposal, in case we have further questions."

Klaus turned around, grabbed Oliver's arm, and hurried him out of the building.

.   .   .

Ten minutes later, Oliver and Klaus were in the car on their way back to the precinct.

"You think the old guy could be the killer?" Oliver wondered aloud.

"He certainly is suspicious."

"Klaus, there is something . . . Emily Richter's article says that the historic killer was called Dietrich Hellenbroich."

"Right, I remember. What are you getting at?"

"The archivist's name is Dietrich Hellenbruch. Doesn't that sound suspicious?"

"Could be coincidence, though. It's not spelled exactly the same—'bruch,' not 'broich.'"

"True. But he also limps with his left leg, just like the historic killer, Dietrich Hellenbroich."

"That does sound like a few coincidences too many, Oliver. Good thinking. Seems we've found our first suspect. Plus those five names on the list!"

XVIII.
Five Hundred Years Ago

Bastian could already see the first bright rays of dawn on the horizon. His limbs were aching, but he felt happy. Wernhart had just returned from checking on the girls at the church and reported that all five were sleeping peacefully in front of the altar. Father Johannes had sent a jug of warm milk with Wernhart, and the two hungry men were indulging in an early breakfast.

They had outwitted Hellenbroich. For safety's sake, Bastian decided they'd hold the fort for another two hours. He was already looking forward to visiting Marie afterward, having a real breakfast with her, and enjoying the rest of the day. He would immediately put into practice his resolution to spend more time with her.

.   .   .

Two hours later they woke the girls and sent them home to their families. Bastian felt confident that they would track down Dietrich Hellenbroich before the next full moon. He already had a plan that included another, more thorough search of every house and every farm in the surroundings of Zons. This bastard had to be hiding somewhere, and Bastian would not rest until he caught him.

Elated, he walked quickly down Rheinstraße toward the Zollturm, knowing Marie would be happy to see him and relieved that he could take a break from the Hellenbroich case.

Quietly he walked up the stairs to the bakery. He heard Marie's father scolding his employees and smiled to himself. Marie's father was considered one of the best bakers in the area. Even noblemen traveled from far away to savor his pastry. He paid his employees well, but in exchange he demanded hard work, day and night. Mistakes were simply not tolerated. Bastian felt happy that his sweetheart was not as severe as her father. He knocked softly at her door.

"Marie, it's me, Bastian. Open the door!"

Nothing. Not a sound came through the wooden door. Although he knew it was not appropriate, he opened the door anyway. Her bed was empty—and untouched. Nobody had slept in there, or so it seemed. Had she gotten up early and left it tidy? Bastian knew this wasn't at all likely; Marie slept in whenever she could.

He ran down into the bakery and asked her father if he knew where his daughter was. The sturdy baker ran to Marie's room, and Bastian saw him stagger before letting out a loud cry of anguish. Marie's father clung to Bastian, tears edging his eyes, and it was all Bastian could do not to stagger and cry out himself. Marie had disappeared!

XIX.
Present

At six o'clock in the morning, Oliver Bergmann was sound asleep and dreaming of Emily Richter. It was summer, and they were strolling along a magnificent white, sandy beach. She turned to him and her pert, smiling face came closer, and closer . . . and just when he was about to kiss her, the loud ringtone of his phone interrupted the delicious dream. Oliver groaned. He didn't open his eyes just yet, instead feeling for the phone on the nightstand and answering.

"Oliver, it's Klaus, and it's urgent. We have another body in Zons. I'll pick you up in five and we'll head to the precinct."

After a short stop at the precinct and an equally short, but brutal, briefing—Hans Steuermark had been furious—Oliver and Klaus were in their car, headed to Zons.

"Yesterday this old guy in the county archive is laughing in our faces and today another woman is dead. We should have taken him into custody then and there!" Klaus banged his fist against the dashboard.

"We don't really have anything substantial against him, other than our gut feeling. Let's take a look at the body and then go straight to the archive."

They had already checked the five names on the list. Besides Emily Richter, two other students had borrowed material about the historic killings. The two remaining persons were employees of the National Library in Berlin. However, since those were interlibrary loans, the detectives didn't prioritize the Berlin trace and concentrated, instead, on the students from the area. The killer was sure to be a local. Berlin was too far away.

Of the two students, one was a woman named Isabelle Kirchner. Because of the brutality of the killings, the police assumed they were dealing with a single, male perpetrator and had therefore focused on the other student, Martin Heuer. Klaus was supposed to interrogate him. So far he had not been able to reach him in person or by phone.

This time the crime scene was at the ferry pier on the Rhine. An elderly woman had found the body early in the morning while walking her dog. Now it was a few minutes past seven, and the Rhine meadows still held the chill of the February night.

In the summer, the Rhine's water could be beautifully blue, but at this time of the year it flowed gray and murky, a thin, hazy layer hovering above the water. Even the grass on the Rhine meadows was more gray than green. Yet despite the bleakness of the wintery day, the landscape, as always, emanated a soothing calm.

Oliver had reread the second part of Emily Richter's article. She had kindly let him have a copy of her final draft, although the text, in which she accurately reconstructed the murder of Gertrud Minkenberg five hundred years ago, would not be published until next week.

Back then the City Guard had found Gertrud Minkenberg's body at this exact spot on the Rhine. She had been tortured, raped, and strangled. After the girl had died, Hellenbroich had tied her onto a large wooden board as if it were a bier and shoved her into the waters of the river. To this day, nobody knew why he had not suspended Gertrud Minkenberg on one of the towers, as one would have expected. This seemed to contradict the discipline Hellenbroich had manifested. He had methodically planned and executed the killings, and the investigators assumed that someone or something must have disturbed him before he could suspend Gertrud as well.

Oliver and Klaus noticed that this time Forensics had already taped off a large area around the site. In fact, the owner of the Rhine Ferry had made a furious phone call to Hans Steuermark early in the morning because he was forced to shut down his business for the entire day. But cars and gawkers were not what Steuermark's men needed. They wanted to avoid photos made public by curious reporters revealing important details, thus complicating their investigations. The public was still waiting for them to present a suspect, but aside from the old limping archivist they were basically groping in the dark.

Maybe they could find something today, something that would clearly establish a link to the archivist. They could definitely narrow down their search to those people who had inside knowledge about the historic murder cases. The first part of Emily Richter's article had only appeared several weeks after the first murder, and the second part had not even been published yet. So whatever the public knew now about the killings, the killer had known well before, and in detail. It seemed unlikely that the killer was from out of state. Most murder victims knew their killers personally, and the perpetrator was most often from the same area. But aside from the old limping archivist—who certainly seemed crazy and strong enough—and the five names on the list, they had nothing.

Oliver stepped closer to the dead woman. As far as he could see, every minute detail corresponded to the Minkenberg murder. A medical examiner came and handed him the woman's purse and ID. This time the killer had not bothered to conceal the identification of the victim. Like Michelle Peters, this victim was fully dressed.

111

Oliver thought about the one important difference between the killings in the past and those in the present. The women in his present-day cases had not been raped—had not even been undressed.

The police psychologist had explained that a copycat killer rarely, if ever, was set off by the same trigger as the original killer. In this case it seemed that, while Hellenbroich was in the grip of religious delusions, the current killer was only interested in re-creating the killings as accurately as possible. But the rape had been a crucial element five hundred years ago. Why, then, did the present-day killer deviate in this matter? Maybe they should really be looking for a female suspect. Maybe that could account for why there was no sign of sexual abuse.

Oliver studied the dead woman's ID card. Her name was Christiane Stockhaus. She lived on Wendestraße and was forty-eight years old. Oliver had to think a moment before he recalled the location of the street. And indeed: Wendestraße led directly to the Mühlenturm, at the southwestern corner of the city wall. Hellenbroich had presumably chosen his victims according to their last names. At least that was what Emily had told him.

He scratched his chin and followed his thoughts. Hellenbroich's first victim had been named Elisabeth Kreuzer, the second victim Gertrud Minkenberg. Their first victim, the woman they had found four weeks earlier, was called Michelle Peters. Her last name didn't match the pattern, if there was one. The same for Christiane Stockhaus: her last name should begin with an *M*, if their killer were actually imitating Hellenbroich. Hmm. Didn't look like too much of a copycat anymore, Oliver thought. There were already two significant departures.

His gut feeling still insisted that the killings were imitations, but how to explain those striking deviations? He simply had to speak with Emily Richter again, and he definitely wanted to see her again. Well, with her name on the list from the county archive, plus her expertise as a journalist who had written about the historic murder cases, he had a strong excuse to get to know her better. That thought made him smile.

"Damn it, are you daydreaming?" Klaus snarled at him.

Oliver flinched and looked up. While he had been lost in his musings, Klaus had been inspecting the corpse. The MEs were already lifting her from the board and placing her into a body bag.

"Lorenz from Forensics is running a check to see if we're dealing with the same filaments on the gown as last time," Klaus informed him.

"I had asked him to test whether they're also identical to the ones we found at the Body in the Woods," Oliver replied, his eyes fixed on the corpse. "Did he say anything about that? I'm still waiting for the results."

"No, no results so far. They sent the sample to the Central Lab. You know, play it safe. They have the better equipment there. Nobody wants to be the one who makes a mistake here."

"Sounds good. Let's head back. But let's stop at Wendestraße 26 on the way. I want to see exactly where the victim lived."

.   .   .

Ten minutes later, Oliver and Klaus were looking at the second victim's house at Wendestraße 26. The house was tiny, very old, but perfectly well preserved, with a wonderful view of the ancient, imposing Mühlenturm less than thirty feet away. They glanced at the nameplate. Christiane Stockhaus had lived there all by herself.

"Should we take a brief look?" Klaus asked.

It was tempting, but Oliver knew they had better wait for Forensics. Hans Steuermark would wring their necks if they forced the door and entered on their own. Oliver suggested they climb the fence instead to get into the small garden behind the house. This wasn't in keeping with police regulations either, but maybe not as bad a violation.

Carefully, they climbed over the fence and, tiptoeing along a small path, reached the rear of the house. Behind the house, entwined in old plants and trees, lay a small garden. Even at this time of year, with the tree branches bare, it was hard to see into it. Oliver noted that the foliage not only kept them safe from prying neighbors but also could have shielded the killer.

A smell of decay hovered in the air. Oliver sniffed and tried to determine where the foul odor was coming from. The smell intensified with each step he took toward the small terrace. Then he noticed that the glass door stood open a crack. The killer had intruded through the terrace door.

"Klaus, come here. I found something!"

Klaus interrupted his inspection of a small shed at the far end of the yard and came quickly over to Oliver.

"You smell that, too?"

"Yep. Smells like rotting garbage that hasn't been emptied out for days."

"Seems like the victim hadn't been home for a while."

"Yeah," Klaus concurred. "The killer either kidnapped her several days ago and had her locked up, or we just found her late. It's possible that she was lying in the Rhine for more than a day."

Oliver nodded. Klaus was right. In the early months of the year, the ferry wasn't that busy, and the cold temperatures could have significantly slowed the body's decomposition. Also, the body had been heavily beaten. They couldn't do much else but wait for the autopsy results. One thing, however, was already clear: Christiane Stockhaus had not left her home by her own will.

. . .

One week later, Oliver and Klaus were still unsuccessfully trying to get hold of Martin Heuer, the student who, according to their list, had borrowed documents from the county archive regarding the medieval killer and his fatal puzzle. Nobody had seen him lately— neither on campus nor at his apartment. Given the circumstances, Hans Steuermark had decided to initiate a missing-persons report for Martin Heuer. That was an hour ago.

While the dean's office knew of an application for a study-abroad semester that had been granted, they didn't know whether and when Martin Heuer intended to leave. Aside from the queer old archivist, Martin Heuer was the only other suspect who could have committed the murders. Isabelle Kirchner, the female student, had produced a watertight alibi when Oliver and Klaus had interrogated her the day before.

XX.
Five Hundred Years Ago

Bastian still couldn't believe it. His dear Marie had disappeared. How could that happen when he himself had implemented every possible security measure necessary to stop Dietrich Hellenbroich? Something must have slipped his attention. But Bastian couldn't think straight, because he hadn't slept in days. If Hellenbroich really had Marie, she was certainly dead by now. A terrible nausea gripped and paralyzed him. Bastian took a deep breath and tried to think harder. And indeed, a tiny flame of hope lit up in his mind: so far, Hellenbroich had made sure to exhibit his victims ostentatiously— yet in this case they still had not found a corpse.

For the umpteenth time, Bastian went through his notes. It was Marie's last name that simply didn't fit into the puzzle: Dünnbier. According to Bastian's theory, the killer should have been hunting for a girl whose last name began with a Z. That was the letter the madman had carved into the wooden door in the Juddeturm. He ran his fingers through his disheveled hair. Then he grabbed the city map of Zons again, along with the map of the stars. The outline of the city wall was identical to the outline of the Raven, only reversed. He turned the drawing of the constellation 180 degrees. Now it matched perfectly the outline of the city wall. The four stars that shaped the Raven sat exactly over the four corners of the wall, where the towers were located. Bastian silently identified each tower by its name. Suddenly, he had an idea.

.   .   .

Marie couldn't see anything. It was pitch-dark and freezing cold, and a dank smell filled the air. Her head was throbbing. She tried to move her hands, but they were tied behind her back with heavy iron chains.

He had put her, chained, into a dark hole. How long would it take until he'd come back and kill her? It was so dark she had lost track of time, unable to tell even whether it was day or night. All she knew was that it couldn't be much longer before he'd come back—and before her short life would be over.

.   .   .

Thanks to the help of the smugglers, Dietrich had easily managed to enter and leave the city undiscovered. In the end he did have to sacrifice his family's amulet, but it had been well worth it. He could always ambush the smuggler and take it back, but he didn't have time for that now. Right now was the time to care for sweet Marie.

He had waited for her in the morning before sunrise and observed her while she walked to the well to get water. On her way back, the two heavy buckets full of water on her shoulders, she had been an easy prey. He had swiftly dragged her to a yard nearby and gradually poured a solid half-gallon of wine down her throat while pinching her nostrils shut. As with the other two girls, this proved to be a miraculous method. Marie had quickly become quiet and obedient. Then he stowed her away in a cart under some potato bags and sneaked her past the guard posts without a problem. His buddy the smuggler distracted the guard, who had no clue that Dietrich was transporting human freight out of the city.

While the girl was sleeping, Dietrich easily chained her up in his secret dungeon. It was located in the vaults deep under the Zollturm and had not been in use for several years. It could only be accessed from outside the city walls. The direct entrance from inside the city fortification had been walled up many years ago, when the city had decided to use the newly built Juddeturm as a prison instead. Since then, the dungeon under the Zollturm had gradually been forgotten. Dietrich had all the time in the world. Nobody would disturb him while he prepared Marie for his nocturnal ritual. Full moon was tonight!

He trembled with arousal and ecstasy as he ran his fingers over Marie's face and neck. She was still asleep. He let his hands rest on her soft, round breasts and felt himself grow hard. It took great self-restraint not to thrust himself between her thighs and take her virginity. He grinned at the thought that he would be the first and last man to enjoy this tender flower. Too bad for Bastian Mühlenberg— this sweet little beauty was his! It was God's will.

But not yet . . . not yet. He had to shave her hair first, and carve his code into her scalp. Only then would he penetrate her and hear her screams. Eventually, he would choke her very slowly and watch her life vanish just as he attained his orgasm. His lecherous thoughts made his hands shake in anticipation. He had to leave quickly and finish the preparations. He would shave her just before midnight, but until then he must remain unseen and find a way to climb the Zollturm. It wouldn't be easy to climb its outside walls. He had done it once, the night Bastian Mühlenberg had surprised him. He wondered whether Mühlenberg now expected him to come climbing up the walls from the outside again, but he dismissed the idea.

Dietrich headed to the farmhouse that had served as his hiding place over the past weeks and sorted through the ropes and pitons for his nighttime ascent. In order to reach the top of the tower in complete darkness, each step had to be planned in painstaking detail. Only the full moon would illuminate his endeavors. Over the past weeks, he had managed to install ten pitons into the walls of the tower. They would help him attach his rope quite easily. Once on the top, he would surprise the guards and knock them out with his special whip. He hoped there wouldn't be more than two soldiers, otherwise he'd have a problem. Once the guards were taken care of, he would drag the unconscious girl to the top via an extralong rope and a winch. Marie, his third victim, represented the brightest star in the Raven, the star closest to its constellation neighbor, Virgo. That's why her physical presence was of the utmost importance for his ritual. Previously, a bowl of blood from his other two victims had been sufficient—and far easier to accomplish, of course. This night would be both Dietrich's most difficult ordeal and his most important achievement.

XXI.
Present

Emily was nervous. Detective Oliver Bergmann wanted to meet her at the Schloss-Café, allegedly to learn more about her research on the historic killer and his fatal puzzle. She thought she had already given him everything she had about the cases. The only thing she herself was still waiting on were the blowups of the last pages in Bastian Mühlenberg's notebook. She needed those prints in order to solve the riddle, and right now she had no additional information for the police. Oliver Bergmann had nevertheless insisted on a meeting, leaving Emily slightly confused, anxious, and flattered at the same time.

She recognized him immediately upon entering the cozy café. He sat bent over one of the tables, deeply immersed in the newspaper. Emily liked the little wrinkles that formed on his forehead while he was concentrating. They added a manly edge to his otherwise quite youthful-looking face. As she approached his table, he lifted his head and a bright smile washed over him. Emily felt magically drawn by his approving gaze and answered with a shy grin.

"I'm reading your latest article in the *Rheinische Post*. Great job!" he said and motioned for Emily to take a seat next to him.

"Thank you. It's basically the same article I gave you. The copy editor made some stylistic changes, but that's all."

"When are you expecting the blowups?"

"Any day now, I hope. I desperately need the last pages from Mühlenberg's notebook for my third part. I've really tried hard to solve the puzzle by myself, but no luck so far."

Oliver's cell phone rang. "Bergmann speaking."

It was the lab. They had finally completed the analysis of the filaments from the body in the forest and the ones from the two dead women in Zons. They were indeed identical. Adrenaline pumped through Oliver's veins. At last they were on to something!

A few days ago, the police had finally located the getaway car from the Body in the Woods case. Although several persons had clearly described it as a Ford Mondeo, investigations had been slow and tedious. Now the car had been found on an abandoned lot in an industrial zone not far from Zons.

Apparently there had been a short circuit in the distributor, and the car had failed the unknown driver. Oliver and Klaus had canvassed every cab company in the broader area, hoping one of the drivers would remember having picked up someone from that spot. This morning they had been lucky: a cabbie from the nearby city of Dormagen had indeed taken a young man from the industrial zone to the Central Station in Dormagen. What was particularly exciting was that the car was registered under the name of Martin Heuer.

The same Martin Heuer who had borrowed documents about the fatal puzzle from the county archive—and who had, by all accounts, disappeared off the face of the earth. Now he had resurfaced, or at least his car had.

While Oliver sat in the café with Emily, Klaus was at the precinct questioning the cab driver for details that might help them identify the cabbie's passenger. Initial clues suggested it could, in fact, have been Martin Heuer. His age, height, hair, and eye color matched perfectly. Still, they could only be certain once the cab driver had positively identified Martin Heuer in a photograph.

"What happened?" Emily asked. She had noticed Oliver's face turning red during the phone call.

"We're looking for a suspect and we just made an important discovery."

"I assume it's about the old guy from the county archive or someone who borrowed the documents?"

"What makes you say that?"

"Well, that old guy is pretty creepy," Emily said, remembering his lascivious stares. "Although it would almost be too obvious. That only leaves someone else with knowledge about the historic cases. The media is already suspecting a copycat killer, someone with access to the archive documents. I bet you've already thoroughly vetted the people who borrowed the material."

"You bet," Oliver answered and locked his eyes with Emily's. "Your name was on the list, too."

"Why, of course!" Emily laughed out loud and went on. "And you have my alibi. My name and Anna Winterfeld's name, right? Wait, no, it must have been Martin Heuer. Anna was on a business trip and Martin Heuer did me a favor and went there to pick up some documents for me."

Oliver swallowed hard when Emily mentioned Martin Heuer's name.

"How do you know Martin Heuer?"

XXII.
Five Hundred Years Ago

After dark, Dietrich Hellenbroich left his hiding place at the farm-house. He was breathing heavily under the load he carried, his left leg dragging behind as usual. In his condition it wasn't easy to transport the many ropes and pitons without losing time or emitting loud groans. His left hand ached. He had hurt himself earlier, while gathering the remaining sharp pitons. The cut was deep and bleeding strongly. He had bandaged the wound, but blood still seeped through the cloth and dripped to the ground in a thin trail, though he hadn't noticed that.

The moon was bright. Despite the gelid February night, Dietrich was sweating under the weight on his shoulders. If he wanted to be done by midnight, he had to hurry up. A rope fell off his shoulder and the pitons rattled to the ground. He ducked down quickly. Damn It! He had to be more careful or he would jeopardize everything. He let a few seconds pass.

Silence. Slowly he gathered the pitons and tucked them tightly to his jerkin. He had two hours left to attach them to the tower wall and carve his symbols in sweet Marie's scalp. He could hardly wait to shave her beautiful long hair and cut *1 8 Z* in her skin. It was a divine miracle that all those beautiful young maidens were there to complete his puzzle.

This time, the pack of wolves came from behind, and quietly. They had followed the trail of his blood and remembered the scent of the human who, roughly a month ago, had killed one of them. Besides, they were ravenous. They split up and formed a half-circle around Dietrich—one wolf to the right, one to the left, and two directly behind the man. Then the leader of the pack jumped and threw Dietrich to the ground. At the same moment, another wolf leaped past Dietrich and attacked him from the front.

On his knees, Dietrich grabbed his knife. But before he could even raise it to sink it into one of the animals, he got tangled up in the ropes, and the leaping wolf aimed for his throat. Nightmarish pain swept through Dietrich's body when the wolf bit a chunk from his neck, severing his carotid artery. His senses faded away before he could even fathom what was happening. Dietrich Hellenbroich's soul vanished from this world without ceremony. The wolves dragged the torn pieces of his body deep into the woods, where they ate their fill. The next day, nothing was left of Dietrich Hellenbroich but a few dispersed bones.

XXIII.
Present

On his way back to the precinct, Oliver got a call from Klaus: Dietrich Hellenbruch, the archivist, had been taken into custody. That morning, Klaus had sent two officers to the county archive to make sure the case-related documents were complete. When the officers began searching through old cardboard boxes, the creepy archivist totally snapped and assaulted one of the officers.

.   .   .

They had desecrated his favorite painting with their dirty hands. He should have handed it over to a museum years ago. He knew that it was an antique and a unique piece, an original oil painting from the fifteenth century depicting a young couple from Zons. To be precise, it showed Bastian Mühlenberg with his fiancée, Marie Dünnbier.

Dietrich Hellenbruch was obsessed with this portrait. The lovers' dramatic story had always touched his heart. It was one of the reasons he had become such an expert in all things related to the historic Zons murder cases.

He would do anything to keep tending this small portrait. He had taken extraspecial care of it by wrapping it in an airtight container and keeping it in the dark to preserve it forever. And now this oaf of a police officer ripped open the archival packaging as if he were dealing with some ordinary book. Dietrich couldn't restrain himself. Furiously, he tried to wrest the portrait out of the officer's hand.

Which was why he was now sitting here in the interrogation room, facing the same two detectives who only recently had gladly listened as he'd revealed the story of the medieval killer and his fatal puzzle. Now they squinted at him as if he had committed a crime. Dietrich let out a deep breath. It didn't make any sense to him. He had helped them, had provided them with a list of names, and in exchange they wanted to steal his most precious possession.

The list of names . . . Deep down inside him, a doubt slowly took shape. Had he really given them all the names? What about the young man who had come by all those months ago, who had been so respectful and eager to learn from him? Had he forgotten to file that man's name because he had been so excited to finally get so much attention?

"Herr Hellenbruch, would you please explain to us why you attacked our colleague?" the younger of the two detectives asked. Dietrich let his head hang down. He was too confused and hurt right now. He wouldn't say a single word. They had stolen his painting!

. . .

It didn't take long for Oliver to realize that they were trying in vain to get information from the old archivist. Their suspect slumped with his head hanging down, entirely tuned out. It almost seemed as if he had fallen into a deep trance. Oliver shook his head. What was that weird old fellow hiding? Was he responsible for the killings after all?

Klaus tried over and over again to make him talk. But after an hour, they had Dietrich Hellenbruch taken back to his cell. They'd have to find another way to uncover the truth.

. . .

The prints had finally arrived! Feeling triumphant, Emily held the large brown envelope in her hands. As fast as she could, she ran up the stairs to her small studio apartment and, out of breath, she locked the door behind her. She closed her eyes. Suddenly she thought about Oliver Bergmann and their meeting last week in the cozy café around the corner. Her fingers dialed his number almost automatically.

"Hi, this is Emily Richter. I've just received the blowups of the pages from Bastian Mühlenberg's notebook. Would you like to look at them with me?"

. . .

Three hours later, Oliver and Emily were sitting again in the cozy Schloss-Café. Oliver knew he shouldn't have knocked off so early. Investigations were still in full swing. After Emily and Oliver had last met, police had expanded their search and were looking not only for Martin Heuer but also for his new partner, Christopher Wörmann.

Their colleagues in Berlin were also now operating on the highest alert level. In the past three weeks, Christopher Wörmann had been seen several times by reliable witnesses in Berlin, which seemed to largely exclude him from the circle of suspects.

Yet Oliver had two crucial arguments for why he didn't want to abandon Christopher Wörmann as a suspect just yet. First there was the distance: while he had initially thought Berlin was too far away, there were, after all, fewer than four hundred miles between the capital and Neuss. By car or train, that ground could be covered in half a day, and by plane in not even an hour. And second, there was Anna Winterfeld, who claimed she had seen Christopher Wörmann several weeks ago in Zons. She had been sitting with Emily in a café and was sure she'd recognized him as he walked past outside. Emily still believed this to be a flight of fancy, but Oliver wasn't ready to dismiss Anna Winterfeld's statement just yet.

He was so deeply lost in his thoughts that he only heard half of Emily's last sentence. He nodded instinctively and followed the movement of her hands, pointing at the table in front of them. She had drawn the city map of Zons and the constellation of the Raven on tracing paper and was now layering one over the other. And then she turned the star map 180 degrees around.

A seasoned expert in deciphering old German handwriting, Emily's cheeks colored with pride and excitement as she read aloud what Bastian Mühlenberg had written in his notebook five hundred years ago. Oliver listened carefully and grabbed a pen. He turned the two maps back to their starting positions and began annotating the corners of the city wall with the letters *K, M, Z,* and *S* respectively. Next to the segments he wrote the numbers *6, 7, 8,* and *9,* according to their lengths. Then he turned the map again by 180 degrees. What he saw left him amazed and astonished.

XXIV.
Five Hundred Years Ago

Bastian shook his head in wonder. He had discovered the truth, the missing piece of the puzzle. Everything made sense now that he had written down the first letters of the names of the four towers.

1 6 K.

Those were the symbols in Elisabeth Kreuzer's scalp. The *6* stood for the shortest segment of the city wall and the *K* stood for Krötschenturm, not for her last name. Why hadn't he seen this connection right away?

Same with the next column: *1 7 M.* Here, the *M* did not represent Gertrud's last name, Minkenberg, but the Mühlenturm that was located at one end of the third-longest segment of the wall, just like the *Z* in *1 8 Z* stood for the Zollturm and the house directly adjacent to it, at the second-longest segment: Marie's house!

Bastian had protected all the girls with a last name starting with *Z* while the killer couldn't have cared less what their names were. He was only interested in where they lived. Damn it! Why, oh why, had he not figured this out earlier? He could have saved Marie!

Desperate, Bastian stood and hurried out the door. Without a clear thought in his mind, he ran through the chill February night until he stopped, out of breath, in front of the Zollturm. He greeted the guards, walked through the city gate to the other side of the wall, and looked long and hard, up along the tower and into the sky.

Bastian raised his fists to the bright, round moon, its waning barely discernible at this point. "Bloody Dietrich Hellenbroich! What have you done to her?"

Suddenly, he saw something black standing out against the wall of the tower. Depending on how he moved his head, it was there and then it wasn't. He walked closer to the wall and saw that climbing pitons had been rammed into the mortar joints of the construction.

"Good Lord! That's why he could surprise me that night on the Zollturm. He climbed up the outer wall!"

Bastian grabbed one of the pitons and with some effort pulled it from the joint. He held it against the light. This piton was made of iron. How could a simple farmer like Hellenbroich afford such a precious material?

Suddenly, Bastian remembered something. Down in the old dungeon under the Zollturm, not only were there chains, but there were also pitons in the mortar joints. The dungeon consisted of one big space, and in order to keep the prisoners from attacking each other or escaping, they had been put in chains hooked to the wall by pitons.

Bastian walked further around the Zollturm. As far as he remembered, all entrances to the old dungeon had been walled up. But when he was standing in front of a heavy wooden door, he saw that it was leaning just a tiny crack open.

Bastian pushed open the door and sneaked inside. It was pitch-dark. The silence was absolute. He could only move forward slowly by groping his way along the wall. Suddenly his foot brushed against a bucket, and it fell over with a clattering noise. Alarmed, Bastian flattened himself against the wall and remained stock-still. If

Hellenbroich was down here, he must have heard the noise. Bastian had to be prepared for anything.

Then he heard a low groaning from the far end of the wall. What was that?

He continued quietly forward, trying to hold his breath. Again he heard the groaning. It was almost inaudible. When his eyes finally adjusted to the darkness, he saw a figure curled on the dungeon floor, arms chained behind her back. A figure he recognized. Marie!

He feared that Hellenbroich had tried to snuff the life out of his beloved as gruesomely as he had from his previous victims. With his heart in his throat and tears in his eyes, Bastian touched the exposed skin near her wrist where the chains had rubbed her skin raw, half expecting—and fearing—to find it cold. Thank God, Marie reacted in panic and defended herself ferociously!

"Marie, sweet Marie, it's me, Bastian. Fear not!"

But Marie acted as if she hadn't heard his words at all; she kept bucking against him until Bastian managed to pull the gag from her throat, and she let out a long, tortured scream that echoed against the walls of the dungeon. Then she fainted. Frantically, Bastian freed her wrists from the chains and carried her out into the fresh air. He put his head on her chest to discern her heartbeat. It was feeble, but it was there! He looked up to the sky and thanked God. He had found her, praise God in Heaven. He had found Marie, and she was alive.

XXV.
Present

So the killer chose his victims on the basis of their locations and not their last names! Aside from the absence of rape, there were no deviations from the historic killings, really. The victims were women who lived in the houses closest to the respective city gates and towers, and the lengths of the wall segments determined the order in which he attacked them. He had begun with the shortest and had intended to work his way up to the longest segment, but never did. What if the current killer wanted to accomplish Dietrich Hellenbroich's incomplete ghastly "masterpiece"? Oliver glanced nervously at the upper-right corner of the city wall.

"Rheinstraße 4. Theoretically, that's where the next victim lives," Oliver said and looked at Emily.

She swallowed hard and her face turned deep red. "It's Anna's house! Oh my God, it's Anna's house!" She jumped to her feet and implored Oliver, "Tonight is the full moon. The killer always attacks at full moon. We need to go to Anna's right now. There's no way she can stay alone in her apartment tonight!"

With trembling fingers, Emily searched the contacts on her phone and called her friend. Damn it, it went straight to voice mail.

The phone was switched off. Panic squeezed her chest and throat. She ran to Oliver's car while he followed her and alerted his partner. She prayed they wouldn't be too late!

.   .   .

Anna was exhausted. Her job at the big Düsseldorf bank was so stressful these days. Many of her coworkers had been home sick with the flu, so their clients' files had landed on Anna's desk. She parked her car in the lot behind the Zollturm and decided to go for a short walk before passing out in bed.

She thought about Martin. It was nuts, all the things that had happened over the past few months. Not only had he suddenly come out as gay, but now he was also a murder suspect, wanted nationwide? Anna still couldn't make sense of it. She had been with this man for many years, had wanted to spend the rest of her life with him, but apparently she hadn't known him at all. Her feet found their way to her favorite bench at the Rhine, and she sat down. She recalled falling asleep here a few months ago and meeting Bastian. He was attractive, kind, and extremely courteous. He seemed to hail from a different world.

She looked up into the night sky, admiring the full moon and the brightness of the stars. Here in Zons, undisturbed by the city lights of Düsseldorf or Cologne, one could still admire the stars in the sky and see how bright they really were.

But enough ruminating when her warm, lovely bed awaited! Anna shivered in the February cold, stood up, and hurried back to her apartment. She had already reached the Zollturm and was fishing for her keys when she saw someone waving at her about twenty yards away. She stopped and took a closer look. It was Bastian.

"Meet me at the Mühlenturm!" she heard him say in a loud stage whisper.

"Why, don't you want to come up and have a cup of tea at my place?" Anna replied.

Bastian shook his head; he had already headed off. "Trust me. See you at the Mühlenturm!"

Anna watched, confused, as he disappeared into the darkness. While she certainly didn't feel like walking through the cold anymore, it seemed like fate that he'd come along just as she was recalling their strange encounter by the Rhine. And she was glad to see him again. So without thinking about it any further, she turned around and headed toward the Mühlenturm.

.   .   .

He peered nervously at his watch. It was late. She should be home by now. Where the hell was she? He groped his way through the darkness of her apartment. He had planned everything so perfectly. As soon as she walked through that door, his trap would snap shut. All the work, planning, and maneuvering he had invested over the months, for just this one moment; the anticipation alone was killing him. So far, everything had worked out just fine. Nobody had seen through him.

"Damn it, where is that bitch?"

Frantically he tore at his brown hair. He was waiting for her behind the door. All he had to do was move in quickly, covering her mouth so that the neighbors didn't hear her scream while he prepared her for his ritual. He would accomplish what had begun in Zons more than five hundred years ago!

Half an hour later he finally heard the building door open. Every muscle in his body tensed up. Adrenaline pumped through his veins. With each step up the stairs, she drew closer to him. A key was inserted in the lock and then twisted. Softly, the door opened and a woman entered. With her right hand, she fumbled for the light switch. But he was prepared and had turned off the fuse.

Just another tiny step closer, you bitch. He held the gag in his left hand and a sharp knife in his right. As if she had heard him and obeyed, she took another step.

Suddenly her neck was squeezed in the crook of someone's arm, and at the end of that arm was a gleaming knife blade. At the same time, the intruder's other hand worked at shoving a piece of cloth into her mouth. Instinctively she turned her head to the side.

In the certainty of having trapped his victim, he groaned triumphantly—but his triumph was cut short when a beam of light shone through the darkness and pooled on his face. For a moment, he was blinded.

"Drop the knife and slowly raise your arms!" a male voice commanded.

Confused, he dropped the knife and held his hands over his head. He was still wondering who could have possibly accompanied Anna home, when the room lit up. Someone had found the fuse box and flicked the power back on.

He blinked at the woman who'd fallen to the floor when he had released his grasp. That wasn't Anna! It was Emily!

.   .   .

Oliver helped Emily onto Anna's couch while Klaus handcuffed the killer. Oliver's first thought had been that it was Martin Heuer, but then a horrified Emily had screamed another name: Christopher. Christopher Wörmann.

The young man seemed just as staggered. He had been waiting for Anna, who just now was stepping through the door to her apartment, her eyes wide.

"Christopher? Emily? What the hell is going on here?" Startled, Anna stood in her door frame and tried to make sense of what she saw. Christopher was handcuffed and stood facing the wall in her living room; a police officer was frisking him. Emily, her face ashen, sat on the couch next to that detective, Oliver Bergmann, who had questioned her about Martin. When Anna entered, everyone looked up at her.

"God damn it, Anna, why didn't you pick up your phone? I've been desperately trying to call you!"

"It wasn't intentional; my battery was dead. What are you all doing in my apartment?"

"He is the killer!" Emily pointed her finger at Christopher.

Christopher stared crazily at Anna. "Do you think the other two made such a scene?" he hissed at her.

"What do you mean, the other two?"

"Oh, think hard for a moment. And just try to imagine how difficult it was for me to get that besotted Martin away from you so I could complete my plan!"

Anna's heart raced up into her throat. "What did you do to Martin, Christopher?"

"What did I do to him? Do you really think we were dating? God, how pathetic you are!"

"Shut your trap this instant. We'll take you to the precinct." Klaus handed Christopher over to two officers who had arrived at the scene. Then he turned to Anna.

"We understand you're confused and upset—you have every right to be. Just give us some time to sort out every detail at the precinct. For now just be happy that you're still alive."

. . .

The next morning, Emily and Anna went to the precinct. After all the commotion, they had both spent the night at Emily's apartment in the student dorm in Cologne. Oliver Bergmann and his partner had given them a ride and made sure they were safe and sound before the detectives headed to the precinct for a first interrogation of their suspect.

In the precinct, Oliver Bergmann was already expecting Emily and Anna. He escorted them into his office. Documents about the Zons murder cases, then and now, were piled high on his desk.

"Well, Frau Richter, I need to pay you my sincere compliments. You have saved your friend's life," he said and smiled shyly at Emily, who already felt he was speaking too formally to her. He looked very much in love.

"We have interrogated Christopher Wörmann through the night," he continued. "He is responsible not only for the murders of Michelle Peters and Christiane Stockhaus, but also for the murder of Martin Heuer. The two women victims fell prey to the same geographic bad luck that doomed the victims Kreuzer and Minkenberg five hundred years ago: they just happened to live where lunatics—separated by five centuries—had set their sights."

Anna wasn't following Oliver's words about the female victims. All she heard were the words "Martin Heuer." She moaned, "My God, Martin is dead?"

Tears welled up in Anna's eyes. *No, please let this not be true.*

"Before you proposed to Martin Heuer in the small café in Zons, Christopher Wörmann had blackmailed him and forced him to reject your proposal. He threatened he would kill you if Martin did not follow his instructions."

Anna recalled how she had mulled over the right words for days before meeting Martin. Christopher had helped her significantly with the proposal during their many telephone conversations.

She had proposed on a beautiful autumn day. Anna had picked the small café in the heart of Zons because it seemed especially fit for this romantic occasion. But as soon as she popped the question, Martin disappeared to the bathroom—and when he came back with a pale face, she knew immediately there was not going to be a wedding. At least not between the two of them! Martin said he needed some time to think, but his answer was visible then and there. Three days passed, and then Martin came out to her as gay. He wanted to spend his life with her best friend, Christopher. The next day, he was already on his way to Berlin with Christopher. Since then she hadn't heard a word from him.

She'd had her heart broken once; it now broke her heart again to learn the truth. What Martin had done, he had done out of love in order to save her!

"Why did Christopher do this?" she asked.

Oliver frowned and embarked on an explanation.

"When Emily Richter began researching the historic murder cases, Wörmann had already developed his mania. When we searched his apartment last night, we found evidence that he had been obsessed with the fatal puzzle and the killer for several months. The officers seized abundant material about the historic events and the solution to the puzzle. The entire apartment was filled with related documents, copies of ones he'd somehow borrowed from the Zons archive without leaving a record of his visit, and others he got on interlibrary loan from Berlin.

"Since he knew how the killer had chosen his victims back then, Wörmann followed suit. You were to be the third victim, because you live in the house where Marie Dünnbier lived. Marie was almost Hellenbroich's third victim.

"Wörmann knew that if you married Martin Heuer, Martin would have moved in with you, and then it would have been extremely difficult to assault you in your apartment. Or you would have moved in with Martin, leaving your place vacant and ruining that crucial piece of the puzzle. So he saw the engagement as something to be prevented at all costs. Initially, his plan seemed to work out. Martin agreed to break up with you. But after three days, Martin Heuer changed his mind and wanted to reunite with you. He was on his way to visit you when Wörmann ambushed him, killed him, carefully burned his fingertips, and discarded him in the patch of forest next to the A57. Now that he has confessed, we can close the file on all those cases. Unfortunately, the missing-persons report wasn't filed until our chief of police issued one, and it took us a long time to identify the Body in the Woods. Otherwise we might have linked the cases far earlier.

"In any event, you should be grateful that you came home so late last night—otherwise he would certainly have killed you. He wanted to complete Hellenbroich's murderous puzzle at any cost. As Emily wrote in her article, and as Christopher must have found in the historic documents, Dietrich Hellenbroich did not manage to sacrifice one girl for each tower—and in the sick logic of his hallucinations, that deprived him of the divine powers of a Lord's Warrior. It seems that Christopher Wörmann worshipped Hellenbroich as a saint of sorts. In his apartment we even came across an altar decorated with old writings and drawings. Apparently he wanted to re-create the atrocities of his idol as faithfully as possible in order to catapult his master to fame and glory once again. He had even returned to Zons to scope out his planned murder sites. It remains to be determined during the trial whether Wörmann is liable for his actions or legally insane. But one way or another, whether in prison or a psych ward, he will be locked away for a long time."

As she took in the detective's explanation, Anna's glance fell onto a photograph. It was a photo of an oil portrait from the 1500s, of a young man and a young woman. Anna recognized Bastian immediately. She grabbed the photo and stared at it.

"Who is this?"

"Bastian Mühlenberg. Five hundred years ago he was doing my job, so to speak. He chased the killer and tried to solve the fatal puzzle. The woman is Marie Dünnbier, his fiancée. Hellenbroich abducted her, but Bastian rescued her."

Anna couldn't believe it. Had she only imagined meeting Bastian Mühlenberg? She was a banker, a job where concrete, rational business was the rule. Each day she demonstrated that she could think clearly. Never in her life had she suffered from hallucinations or any mental instability. And yet she could have sworn that Bastian Mühlenberg had stood in front of her in the flesh.

Anna was at a loss. She looked over to Emily, who shrugged her shoulders helplessly. It was the strangely formal man named Bastian who had delayed Anna's arrival at her home. She had waited for over an hour at the Mühlenturm and was bitterly disappointed when Bastian didn't show up. Had he not diverted her there, she would have gone straight home and to her certain death. Whether it was real or imaginary, it didn't matter. Bastian Mühlenberg had saved her life!

XXVI.
Five Hundred Years Ago

The sails of the mill were buzzing in the wind. Many months had passed since Bastian had rescued Maric from the dungeon. Now he was idling in a meadow in the sunshine and chewing on a blade of grass. He was very pleased with himself. They may not have arrested Hellenbroich, but they had thwarted his megalomaniacal master plan and prevented more killings in Zons.

Bastian leaned back on his elbows and blinked at the hot summer sun when he suddenly heard a loud humming nearby. His comfortable quiet disturbed, he sat up reluctantly and looked in the direction from which the roaring noise seemed to come. Startled, he sat up. He couldn't believe his eyes.

To be continued . . .

Author's Afterword

Dear Reader,

I want to thank you for purchasing and reading *Fatal Puzzle*. I hope that you have spent some entertaining, suspenseful hours with my first book.

All the places that I describe in the thriller do exist in reality. The map that I drew and that you can find at the very beginning of the book shows you the historic city center of Zons. Should you ever come and visit our medieval town, this is exactly what you will find. They have a similar map at the tourist information center across from the regional museum, at Schlossstraße.

Most locals of Zons refer to Burg Friedestrom as "Castle Friedestrom." I guess it is because they prefer to have a castle rather than a fort. Also, the street running right in front of it is called "Schlossstraße" (Castle Street), not "Burgstraße." I have, however, chosen to stick with the official name.

Some readers have asked why I refer to four towers in Zons; the city map only indicates three. If you count the Schlossturm at the southeastern corner of the wall, you have four towers in four corners.

The origin of the name Krötschenturm is uncertain. In old German, "Krötsch" meant something like "sickly," which is why people assume that in times of the plague and other epidemics, the sick were locked in that tower to keep them away from the healthy population. It's also possible that the tower got its name from the surrounding gardens, the so-called Kreuzgärten. That's actually the field's name to this day. "Creutzthurm" could have become "Creutzschturm," and then "Krötschenturm." Unfortunately, there aren't any preserved documents to answer this question.

There is no historically proven connection between the constellation of the Raven and the layout of the city wall. I simply happened upon this similarity while I was researching and took the artist's liberty to create the code based on this coincidence. However, historic events mentioned in the book, like the authorization to levy customs tolls granted to Zons by Archbishop Friedrich von Saarwerden of Cologne, did indeed take place.

The characters in my book are fictional and invented. I cannot rule out that one or another character might bear a certain resemblance to persons living today—however, this is not intentional.

Should you have questions about my book or if you would like to send me your personal feedback, you are welcome to contact me via email at contact@catherine-shepherd.com.

Yours,
Catherine Shepherd

About the Author

Thriller author Catherine Shepherd was born in 1972 and lives with her husband in the medieval town of Zons on the river Rhine, the setting for her first book, *Fatal Puzzle*.

After graduating from a German high school, Shepherd, who uses a pen name, studied economics and went on to work for a major German bank for many years. Having started writing as a teenager, she dedicated herself to writing seriously in 2011 and published her first thriller in April 2012. It didn't take long for her e-book *Fatal Puzzle* to hit #1 on the German Amazon bestseller list, under the title *Der Puzzlemörder von Zons*.

Her second thriller was released in March 2013 under the German title *Der Sichelmörder von Zons*, and in December 2013, Shepherd published her third book, *Kalter Zwilling*.

For more information about the author and her thrillers, visit her website at www.catherine-shepherd.com or check her out on Facebook at www.facebook.com/Puzzlemoerder and www.facebook .com/catherine.shepherd.zons or you can find her as @shepherd _tweets on Twitter.

About the Translator

Julia Knobloch is a translator, writer, and producer. She has been living in the US for four years and translates fiction and nonfiction for AmazonCrossing and individual clients. *Fatal Puzzle* is her first fiction translation from her native German to English. Julia's documentaries on explorers, adventure expeditions, and WWII history have aired on the National Geographic Channel, Discovery Channel, ABC, and German public broadcasting. Her writing has appeared in major German and Argentine newspapers and magazines and online with Open Democracy and The Brooklyn Rail. She lives in Brooklyn and has just finished her first poetry manuscript.

Made in the USA
San Bernardino, CA
16 July 2018